GRIM

GRIMALKIN'S TALES

Strange and wonderful cat stories

by

STELLA WHITELAW

JUDY GARDINER

MARK RONSON

St. Martin's Press
New York

Library of Congress Catalog Card Number 85-50220

ISBN 0 312 35057 0

First U.S. Edition

10 9 8 7 6 5 4 3 2 1

CONTENTS

1. THE CAT THAT COULD FLY by Stella Whitelaw   7
2. IN MY GRANDMOTHER'S HOUSE by Judy Gardiner   19
3. STRAUSS by Mark Ronson   34
4. NINE LIVES by Stella Whitelaw   49
5. THE BAD LUCK CAT by Judy Gardiner   58
6. TICO by Mark Ronson   70
7. ARBUTHNOT ROAD by Stella Whitelaw   86
8. GERSHWIN by Judy Gardiner   102
9. SMOKEY by Mark Ronson   115
10. THE GREAT GOD MAU by Stella Whitelaw   128
11. CATS DO MAKE A HOME, DON'T THEY?
    by Judy Gardiner   138
12. SAMKIN by Mark Ronson   147

The Cat that could Fly

Stella Whitelaw

It began on a curiously still morning when not a leaf stirred and even the butterflies seemed to hover over the flowers without moving. The dead elm stretched its ashen branches skywards waiting for the chop that was a long time in coming. A mile up a chartered Tri-Star ferried yawning early starters to a package holiday in Majorca, its gentle hum followed by vapour trails in the sky.

Leopold trod the dew-hung clover with delicate paws. He was a big ginger and white cat with a wide, surprised face and fluffed cheeks. His eyes were very green and brilliant which added to his startled look. He lived an uncomplicated life; he ate and slept; he caught the occasional bird or shrew just to keep his hand in.

The family that he lived with were what Leopold called sleek. They had everything – two cars, two colour television sets, a video recorder, wall to wall stereos, a deep freeze that could take a whale, every domestic appliance on the market, and yet they were as mean as a cross-eyed snake. They bought him unbranded cat food, a mish-mash of wet cereal and unmentionable animal parts; he never got a taste of fresh liver or fish. They drank the cheapest coffee, bought broken biscuits, and cut all the tenpence-off coupons out of the paper. They were sleek all right.

They were sleek on affection too. If Leopold jumped onto a vacant lap, he was hastily brushed off.

'Gerroff my suit! I don't want your hairs all over me. Shoo. Shoo,' said the sleek man impatiently.

The sleek woman was as bad. Her clothes were also uncatable. The one person who liked Leopold was the daughter, Dana, but she was pre-occupied with O levels and boy friends, and the only time Leopold saw her was when she came in late from a disco and they shared the cosy quietness of a 2 am kitchen.

As Leopold took his early morning stroll down the garden, he heard a faint chirp chirp. The sound made his stomach contract. He was hungry. Last night's supper was best forgotten, and they would not give him a breakfast until he had been outside for at least an hour. Leopold did not understand these rules. It was another of their odd ways. He noticed that they ate broken biscuits whenever they felt like it.

Leopold crept up on the sound. It was a baby thrush, softly speckled brown and white, a big fluffy helpless creature, looking straight at Leopold with bright, trusting eyes. It staggered a few inches and fell forward onto its plump breast. Leopold's surprised expression sharpened with delight. This was obviously some sort of game. He patted the soft feathers with a tentative paw. The bird chirped encouragingly and hopped another few inches. A few trees away, the mother bird heard her baby's call but was not alarmed. It had to learn to fly by itself.

Suddenly Leopold pounced. The baby's neck hung limp between his jaws. Leopold growled, a low rumbling jungle sound echoing back from his wild ancestors. He paraded his victim, the feathers stuck out round his mouth like an air force moustache. He crunched the tiny body thoughtfully, blood on the short white fur under his nose.

The mother bird went crazy. She flew from branch to branch in distress. She swooped over the ginger cat and what was left of her baby, her cries loud and distraught. But it was too late. There was nothing she could do. She took one last look at the big cat and flew blindly into the empty air.

There was a great oak which Leopold liked to climb. He never went very far because he knew his limits. But today the baby bird lay heavily in his stomach, and Leopold climbed higher, hoping to leave the uncomfortable feeling behind. The thick tangled branches gave no hint of how high he was climbing. He went on, up and up, leaping from one claw-hold to the next. Because there was no wind, the branches barely moved, again giving Leopold an unfounded sense of security. When a broken branch revealed a glimpse of the land below, Leopold was quite amazed. He could see the tops of other trees, padded with green-like cushions beneath him. The garden of

8

his house was a smudge of blurred colours. In the distance was the church spire, almost eye level. A helicopter whirled into sight, coming straight towards the oak, its rotor blades clattering discordantly.

Leopold leaped back. He forgot he was on a branch, up a tree. He took off backwards, falling head between heels, somersaulting through a cascade of leaves and broken twigs, the wind rushing through his whiskers, flashes of sky and earth alternately in vision as he hurtled towards the ground.

He spread his paws helplessly in a gesture of supplication to the great cat god in the sky. He closed his eyes tightly. He did not want to see what was coming to him.

Leopold first became aware of a change when the swift rushing wind in his ears slowed to the merest whisper. He was still falling, but no longer that shattering, pummelling plunge earthwards. He seemed to be drifting. Perhaps he had died.

He opened one eye the merest slit. He saw the Japanese maple, a beech hedge and below him a bed of button dahlias, prim and tight-headed. He landed right in the middle of the flowers and shook himself.

'Gerroff my dahlias!' the sleek woman yelled from a bedroom window.

Leopold extracted himself from the damaged flowers with dignity and walked away, a curled yellow petal behind one ear like a Hawaiian hula dancer. He had too much to think about to be worried by appearances.

After breakfast he sat looking at the oak tree. It did look very high. What had happened to him? How could he have fallen all that way and survived? He knew that cats could fall from the roof of a house and land unhurt on four paws, but that tree was at least three houses high, or so it seemed to Leopold. Eventually Leopold wandered into the wood to the far end where it was secluded and the blackened stump of a tree struck by lightning stood lonely and unloved.

He climbed the black stump, sniffing the lingering smell of sulphur. He sat in the fork and looked down on the carpet of pine needles below. It was about eight feet high. He could either scramble down the charred bark, or he could jump.

He jumped. He expected to land on the bed of needles in about one and a half seconds flat. But strangely he seemed to float. It took four seconds to land. It was puzzling.

He thought about it for a time, then decided to climb the stump again. He jumped off from the fork. This time it took six seconds and he landed some yards away on dry bracken.

Leopold was beginning to enjoy himself. After all, what harm was there if he wanted to spend the afternoon jumping off an old tree? What the hell! He climbed again, rapidly, like a red arrow. He jumped again, quite merrily, paws spread, wondering where he would land.

Suddenly he saw a clump of nettles right below him. Despite his thick fur, he knew all about nettles. His pink nose was particularly vulnerable. He stretched wide his paws in horror and sailed over the top of the clump. Without thinking, he lifted both his right legs and wheeled away in a shallow curve towards an open patch of ground.

When he returned that evening, the family scolded him and said he was too late for supper. They sat round the television, dunking broken biscuits into watery coffee. Leopold licked at the dried bits still stuck on his breakfast saucer. His drinking bowl had not been changed and the water was practically growing algae. He jumped on the draining board and stretched his neck towards a dripping tap.

'Gerroff the draining board, you wicked cat,' the woman shouted. Leopold obligingly removed himself. For a split second, as he jumped, he almost spread his paws but an inner caution stiffened this action and he landed awkwardly, unbalanced.

'Now don't do that again! I won't allow it.'

He sat on the front steps in the dark until Dana came home from her date. She was sniffing into a twisted scrap of handkerchief and her mascara had run into panda smudges. She made herself a mug of milky cocoa and poured a large saucerful for Leopold. She knew where her father kept a hidden packet of chocolate biscuits and she helped herself, spreading out the remainder so that he would not notice the difference.

'Of course, I can never tell them about Roger,' she said to the cat, stroking his ears. 'They wouldn't understand about him not having any money, or a job. They'd never understand.'

Leopold daintily mopped up the fallen crumbs. No, they would never understand. The next morning, he was at the door, waiting to be let out, and streaked through the moment there was a crack. He spent all day practising, graduating from tree to taller tree. It was exhilarating. By mid-afternoon, he acknowledged what he had been wondering about ever since his miraculous escape from the big oak.

It was not simply this new skill which filled him with joy and excitement, but the fact that it held the key to something far more important – escape. He walked back to the house quite jauntily, not caring that his supper would not make up for missing breakfast.

'Caught yourself a little mouse for breakfast, did you?' asked the sleek woman, scraping the last globule of mush from the tin. 'There's a good pussy.'

Good pussy swallowed the revolting food. It was important now to keep up his strength. When he saw the family go out for the evening, he climbed onto the roof of the house, skirting the television aerial and leaping up onto the flat top of the chimney. He sat there for a long time, his tail neatly curled over his feet. It was not that he lacked courage; it was just that this was the first time he had contemplated jumping from anything other than a tree. And it might be that trees were a vital ingredient . . . however, he would never find out just by sitting.

He stepped off into space, automatically widening his paws, claws out-stretched, tail stiffened, lifting his head. These movements slowed his free fall, then he leaned carefully into a wide arc, his brilliant eyes almost crossed with concentration. He glided across their garden, passed the dahlias, rising over the hedge, then soaring up as he came face to face with an overgrown rhododendron bush. The evening air was cool and peaceful as he locked into a pure straight calculated climb, his whiskers twitching as the wind resistance began to increase. He winked as he passed two alarmed starlings flying home to roost. As he topped the climb, he closed his paws, tucked his head down and streamlined his descent onto the flat roof of a neighbour's garage. Shaking with relief, he sat down and began to lick back his ruffled fur. He had done it. He did not need a tree.

After that, there was no stopping Leopold. He jumped off anything and everything. His greatest day was when he managed to climb into the church belfry and then up the narrow ladder that was steel-pinned to the side of the spire. There was precious little room

11

at the top for him and the weathervane. The dim metal cock spun round, creaking, obviously out of control, almost knocking Leopold off his perch. Leopold took off in a perfect swallow, levelling out at about a hundred feet without any effort. The thermals of air took him up higher and he gloried in the feeling of space and freedom. Below the neat rows of houses and gardens stretched for miles. Dark green patches of woodland were all that were left of the great forests which had once covered the hills. He flew over the top of the ugly grey gasometer, tracking for fun the snake-like train that swayed along the line. People were so small, wobbling along on matchstick legs, heads down, wrapped up in their worries and dreams. No one noticed a large ginger and white cat flying casually overhead.

He began to get more adventurous, exploring the countryside and neighbouring towns. He followed the river Thames to London, but did not stay long among the high-rise flats and skyscraper office blocks. The air traffic bothered him and the pigeons were rude.

'I've just seen a cat fly by,' said a stunned window cleaner in a cradle at the 21st floor of some offices.

'Fell out a winder,' said his pal morosely, wiping a dark mirrored pane of glass. 'Probably pushed.'

'It was flying. It was a ginger cat.'

'We gotta little tabby. Company for the missus.'

The window cleaner screwed up his eyes against the sun. Whatever it was was almost out of sight, skimming over the top of St Paul's dome, the cross sparkling in the bright rays. Perhaps it was a ginger bird. He clamped his mouth shut and turned back to his work. He did not want to get his cards.

Of course, Leopold could not keep his secret forever. He began to get careless. The family gave a party with watered gin and cut-price whisky to celebrate the sleek man's latest promotion. As they cleared up, Leopold slid among the chairs looking for morsels of cocktail snacks. If they were anything like the general standard of catering in the house, most of the guests would have dropped them. He found a pathetic shrimp on a soggy toast finger stuffed behind a pot plant. It wasn't bad. The cheese they had used had been so stale and crumbly, it had parted company from the cubes of pineapple and there were lots of bits on the floor.

The sleek woman had also lashed out on a dip made from dried chicken soup and tinned cream. Not many people had dipped so there was a lot left. As she was scraping it all together and wondering if she could turn it back into soup, a big dollop slopped off her finger and fell onto the carpet. Leopold raced to the rescue.

'Gerrout the way! You damned cat! Look what you've made me do,' she stormed. She swiped at him with her morocco bound visitors book. (Someone had signed: 'Unbelievable party, darling.')

The book caught Leopold on the side of his head. Swift as a flash he spread his paws and leaped to the safety of the pelmet. The woman was furious and did not notice anything unusual about the ascent. She lashed out at him again and he took off, flying right across the room to a shelf on the other side.

'You wicked thing,' she shrieked, wondering if she had watered the gin enough.

'Mummy,' said Dana, opening the french doors to let out the smoke-laden air. 'I think Leopold can fly.'

Leopold soared out into the night air. He shared a gnarled oak with an old owl and contemplated the future. They knew now. Perhaps it would not matter. After all, what could it possibly mean to them? Habit was hard to break and at breakfast time, Leopold nodded to the sleepy owl and took off for home. He flew down into the garden and sauntered up to the back door, casually twitching his tail.

'Darling,' cooed the woman, scooping him into her arms. 'Darling Leopold, you've come back to mummikins! Nice pussy, come and have some lovely milk.'

Leopold was thoroughly alarmed, squashed against her second best jumper with the sequin buttons. She smelled of musk and face cream. He struggled but she was holding him very tightly. He heard the back door shut and it was the thud of doom.

They sold him to a circus. As he was being driven away in the back of the circus owner's Cortina estate, the sleek family were hugging each other with glee, waving the fat cheque and planning to buy more cars, more televisions and a holiday in the Bahamas.

Leopold quite liked the circus for about two days. They put him in a large cage that smelt of bear, and people came and looked at him, bringing delicious things like fish and chips, beefburgers and anchovy pizzas.

13

Then the circus owner put him on the scales and declared a diet. Leopold must not gain a single ounce. Aerodynamics he called it.

Leopold did not understand the circus. It was so bright and noisy with strange animals growling in the night. They did feed him better food than he was used to, though he suspected it was left over from the lion's share.

The trouble started when Miss Dora, the trapeze artist, refused to carry Leopold up the ladder to her platform high in the roof of the big tent. She absolutely refused even to touch him.

'I shall come out in a rash all over,' she said, every rhinestone on her brief costume quivering with indignation.

The circus hands rigged up a basket affair in which to hoist Leopold up to the platform. Leopold hated it. He felt sick as it swayed and jerked higher and higher up into the dim black regions of the roof. He stepped out onto the narrow platform and looked round politely. It was very high up indeed. Miss Dora stood as far away from him as possible.

'Shoo, shoo,' she said, her feathered headdress nodding with each word. 'Go away.'

Someone switched on a spotlight, blinding Leopold. He stepped sideways to avoid the brilliant white light, and disorientated, he fell off the platform. He fell, paralysed with fear, like a stone, and landed with a bounce in the safety net, all four paws and his head stuck through the mesh; it was very undignified.

'Now, Leopold,' said the circus owner, speaking slowly and deliberately. 'When you get up there on the platform I want you to fly across to the other platform.' Leopold looked back at him with puzzled green eyes. 'Fly across, like Miss Dora. Only you're a clever pussy and you don't need a trapeze bar.'

Miss Dora scowled. 'I don't like sharing my act with a cat. It's ignominious.'

Again Leopold was put into the elevator and swung up to the platform. Again he fell into the net. The sweat began to come out on the owner's brow. He had gambled a fortune.

This time Leopold rolled over and got into such a mess in the netting they had to cut it to get him out. He tried not to look smug as he returned to his cage.

'Please, pussy,' said the circus owner the next day, wringing his

14

hands. 'Fly for me. I gotta lotta money tied up in you. You wouldn't want to see old Joss go bankrupt, would you?'

Miss Dora had covered her body thickly with an antibite ointment in order to protect herself from Leopold's deadly rash. The smell was awful. He couldn't stand it for two seconds. He launched himself off the platform at speed, did two fast circuits of the arena, then spotting the exit sign, made a bee-line for the opening. He dipped stylishly over the big top before heading off towards the far country. He felt the faintest twinges in his paws as he climbed higher in the sky. He had never reached this altitude before. His tail streamed out behind him, his fur filled with air and the loose flaps of skin under his armpits belled out like a parachute.

Leopold was looking for the sea. He had had in mind for some time to learn to fly properly. He was a bit afraid of going to the mountains to find an eagle or a condor. They were so big and unpredictable. But seagulls, now they were a different kettle of fish. And there was no doubt about it, they could fly. Leopold's capacity would be one of an ardent observer.

He was quite surprised when he eventually found the sea. It was not at all as he had expected, just miles and miles of heaving wet blue waste. But the seagulls were there in their thousands, screeching and diving and squabbling among themselves. Leopold particularly admired their precision take-offs and landings on water.

He went down onto the pebble beach to practise a few low level take-offs, but each time he nose-dived straight into the sea. It was horrid, and he soon discovered that he could not fly very well if his fur was wet.

'Scram, scram,' shrieked the seagulls as Leopold went headlong into the waves yet again. He gathered his dignity round him like a wet bathrobe and climbed into the heather to dry off.

When he found the cliffs, he knew he had the answer. Their sheer height was impressive; the grandeur of the craggy rock face filled Leopold with quivering pride. This was going to be his home. He was going to be a cliff cat; he saw himself leaping about the rock face as sure-footed as Tarzan, catching his food among the gorse on the headland, sleeping in a small cave. He could watch the seagulls all day and learn their secrets. He would practise diligently from his cliff-top take-off, experimenting, and adapting their flight to his. It

15

was going to be wonderful.

The seagulls were a bit alarmed by this peculiar flying ginger thing. They knew cats ate birds but what sort of cat was this? They resorted to a Mafia style protection racket, dropping Leopold the odd freshly caught mackerel in return for paws-off. This suited Leopold admirably. He did not fancy a mouthful of wet feathers.

Leopold ate well. Fresh fish, rabbits and mice; the dew to drink from fragrant morning puddles shot with silvery sunshine. He was very happy.

His flying improved. He could stay in the air for much longer and with a lot less effort. He could glide in for touch-down with fanatical precision. He experimented with stalling in the air, letting himself fall, heart in mouth, then pulling himself out of it moments before hitting the waves. He skimmed along the surface of the sea with carefree abandon. He learned to loop the loop, to power dive like a blazing meteor; he perfected a victory roll, coming out of it to soar up into the blue sky until everything was so transluscently blue that he could no longer tell which was sea and which were the heavens.

He was sailing along on one such routine flight, his thoughts to himself, when he discovered he could no longer see land. He circled around, his green eyes searching the horizon. He could see nothing solid or familiar. He flew slowly, wondering in which direction to make tracks. He had no idea how far this sea stuff went.

He began to get tired, flying in ever wider circles. Then he realised that the sun had gone and it was getting darker. He was not alarmed by this as he could see very well in the dark. But this was not the night. It was another kind of foreboding grey gloom; the gathering of thunder clouds laden with rain.

Leopold looked up as he heard far-off rumbling. There was going to be one heck of a storm, and he was going to be caught in it. He knew what would happen when his fur got wet. He knew what would happen if he had to land on water. Zwat. Caput. End of Leopold.

He flew on bravely, his body aching. The first big drop of rain hit him squarely between his eyes. He blinked and adjusted his speed. He had to keep his head or this thing would beat him.

He tried to climb higher to get above the storm but it was too late. The thunder clouds were dark and menacing; flashes of lightning lit up the rolling masses of horror. He began to wish he had stayed with the circus, or perhaps even the sleek family.

The storm gathered into a seething black mass overhead; the rain began hitting him like sledgehammers. In minutes he was soaked, his fluffy fur plastered to his skin. He lifted his head, trying to maintain height. Fiercely Leopold fought to hold his own, relying on the months of practising to come to his aid now. But he was losing speed and losing height. The dark water below was surging in great white frothed waves, deep gullies sucking and swallowing each other. One bedraggled ginger and white cat would soon disappear beneath that hungry sea.

Leopold could hardly see now. His lids were glued by the on-slaught of rain. He began to fall. As he fell, he mewed piteously . . .

'Jumping Jehova, if it isn't raining cats and dogs! There, my fine fellow, don't struggle. Mike Kelly's got you safe enough.'

Leopold found himself caught by strong arms that took the impact of his fall. It was a miracle. He must have fallen straight into the arms of a saint.

The saint was wearing glistening yellow oilskins and a brimmed sou'wester off which the rain was dripping. His lined and crinkled brown face had a pair of the bluest eyes Leopold had ever seen.

'And where did you come from? I suppose you done drop out of one of them aeroplanes? My word, we'd better take you down below and dry you off before you catch your death.'

Mike Kelly carried Leopold down into the tiny cabin and began to rub his coat with a rough towel. It was the smallest room Leopold had ever seen, cat-sized in fact. He looked around with interest. The room pitched and rolled in the strangest way, but it did not seem to disturb the man so it must be all right.

'Well, you're stuck here now,' Mike Kelly went on. 'Whether you like it or not. I'm sailing round the world and I shan't make landfall for weeks. You can get off then if you want to, or you can come back to Ireland with me. Please yourself. I'm easy. What do you think?'

Leopold had already made up his mind. No one had ever con-sulted him before, or treated him as an equal.

'I'm needing a ship's cat and a bit of company,' said Mike, opening a tin of evaporated milk. 'So you dropped in just right. You'll earn your keep and I reckon we'll get on . . .'

17

It was the beginning of a lifetime of devotion and mutual companionship. Leopold sailed all over the world with Mike, following him round strange foreign places and wintering sometimes in Southern Ireland in Mike's cottage while his catamaran was docked for repairs or maintenance, and the next voyage was planned.

The circus owner sued the sleek family for misrepresentation and the wrangling went on in court for years. Eventually the judge dismissed the case, saying it was useless to go on when neither party could produce the evidence (ie the cat) in question. The costs were enormous and the sleek family, who had spent the cheque, were rather silent as they made an appointment to see their bank manager. Dana did not go. Instead she ran off with Roger and went to live with him in a caravan.

Leopold did not entirely give up flying, though it took him some time to get his nerve back after that terrible storm. He made sure he did not fly too high, or too far away, realising that navigation was his weak point. He even perfected a new technique of a low level approach for a deck landing.

If Mike ever noticed his cat flying round the masthead, he was too tactful to mention it. Occasionally he was heard to mutter unsaintly comments about the Blarney Stone, or wonder if it was the Irish whiskey.

One day he vowed he'd write a book about Leopold, but then, who would believe him?

In My Grandmother's House

Judy Gardiner

I spent the spring of 1928 in a children's isolation hospital suffering from diphtheria. The occupant of the cubicle next to mine died of it, but I was too worried about my own future to notice her absence overmuch. I had heard that when you had diphtheria they had to slit the side of your neck open to prevent you from choking and I didn't want that to happen. To be slit open, I mean. I would sooner have choked and died like poor Beryl.

But the only thing they did was to give me a lumbar puncture, and I lay day after day staring through the window and trying to pretend that I was King Arthur or someone. As the owner of a rampant imagination I normally spent a lot of time being someone else, but somehow the glass and starch of the isolation hospital discouraged fantasy. No one was allowed to visit us, although one Saturday afternoon a brightly smiling woman waved at me through the window. I had never seen her before, and when she realised that she was smiling at the wrong child her smile fell off and she hurried past.

It was May before I was declared cured and released from custody. The world outside seemed to have become strangely noisy and strenuous, and it was discovered that lying in bed for so long had made me grow like a weed. A weed with a lingering aura of carbolic and ether.

'You need building up a bit,' my father said. 'Country air and good food, so we've decided to send you down to your grandmother for a while.' Although my mother had been dead for two years he still spoke in terms of we and us.

I had only the vaguest memory of my grandmother and didn't particularly wish to go and stay with her, but children argued less in 1928 and two days later he drove me down to Surrey. We stopped for lunch on the way and he encouraged me to have two helpings of pudding.

We arrived when the sky was turning pale evening green. He took my suitcase off the dickey seat and handed me the box of chocolates we had brought for my grandmother.

'I don't want to stay here.' I said it resignedly, but it was like the dread of having my neck slit open all over again.

'You'll have a lovely time,' he said. 'I used to adore this place when I was a boy.'

We walked up the steps to where my grandmother was waiting.

'Look,' she said. 'Katinka has come to meet you!'

Katinka. And my mind goes back to that still May evening with my father in a brown suit and trilby; to the bullnosed Morris on the drive in front of my grandmother's house, and there, standing by her side, a small and impeccable silver tabby with tail held politely aloft.

Even after all this time it still hurts to touch the memory of her; I find myself dabbing at it like someone afraid of being burned. Silver grey mackerel stripes and a pair of cool green eyes and that's enough, that's enough. I make myself write her name, but something in me still cries out at the recollection of what happened.

My grandmother's house was called Riverside Lodge, two sides of its garden being bounded by a tributary of the Thames. The house itself was redbrick and commodious, and had a black and white marble floor and a lead tank wherein grew a Sacred Lily of the Nile. I was introduced to it as if it were a person.

The rooms of the house, lit by a pleasantly subaqueous light filtering through half-drawn holland blinds, were crammed with treasures that spoke of the energetically enquiring Victorian mind. Cases of shells, pebbles, fossils, birds' eggs, all meticulously catalogued. A collection of snuff boxes, musical boxes, boxes within boxes, puzzles, games, Japanese fans, stuffed animals and a bullet removed from the hipbone of a Crimean soldier by the very fingers of Miss Nightingale herself.

I have no recollection of saying goodbye to my father or of watching him depart. After my previous apprehensions I must surely have felt at least a twinge of regret, but I can only remember the delight of exploring Riverside Lodge, of passing awestruck and fascinated from one room to another. A lifesized *papier-mâché* figure of a negro boy in a red stocking cap stood at the bend of the staircase and on the upper landing I discovered a baby's basinette with thin spidery wheels and bodywork made of intricately woven cane. My grandmother told me that my Uncle Arthur had fallen out of it when left unattended and that the resultant dent in his forehead had most probably accounted for his inability to qualify for Sandhurst later on.

I was taken down to the kitchen to meet Mrs Penney, who had been cook-housekeeper to my grandmother for thirty years. Mrs Penney had dimples in her elbows and addressed my grandmother as Mmm, and my grandmother told me that if I wanted anything she was the person to ask.

For supper I had a soft-boiled egg and home-made bread and butter and a glass of milk while my grandmother sat at the opposite end of the dining table peeling an apple.

She was of a delicate build, with meagre white hair frizzed on her forehead and with large eyes faded to a pale tobacco colour. Her skin looked very soft, and was blotched with brown marks that gave her a pleasingly tortoiseshell look, and her skirts came down to her ankles. She always seemed to smile when she spoke, but her voice was so quiet that considerable attention was required if her words were not to be lost.

I wanted to talk to her but didn't know what she'd like me to say. Small, gentle and speckled, I liked her very much but nevertheless remained mute. So she asked me general questions about school and home and then, whether I had any hobbies. I couldn't explain about liking to pretend being other people, so said that I didn't think so.

'I have a great many,' she said, and at that moment the cat Katinka walked silently through the open door and without glancing at either of us went over to the window and curled up in a low chair.

'Katinka sometimes likes to spend the evening in the dining room,' my grandmother said. 'Then at bedtime she goes into her basket in the kitchen.'

I wanted to ask what else Katinka did. As the only cat in a large quiet house I wondered how she filled her days. But my grandmother coiled her apple peel into a tidy little heap at the side of her plate, touched her brownish lips with her table napkin and departed.

'Goodnight, my dear,' she said from the door. 'I hope you will have a restful night.'

She didn't say anything about coming to tuck me up. My mother had always done that, and my father had carried on the tradition, yet I don't remember feeling lonely or homesick on that first evening of going to bed by myself. Someone, presumably Mrs Penney, had unpacked my suitcase and laid my nightdress on the pillow and my sponge-bag on the marble-topped table in the bathroom next door. I climbed up into bed and fell asleep reading the copy of *A Peep Behind the Scenes* which had been thoughtfully left on the bedside cupboard together with a carafe of water, a china box filled with mint humbugs and a jug of columbines. The magic of the place had already enfolded me.

And time slipped by with the quiet ease of the river that bounded the garden. Sometimes my appearance at breakfast coincided with my grandmother's, but on other occasions she had already departed and I had only her neatly rolled table napkin for company. Occasionally I was told that she was having breakfast in her room.

I didn't mind. After the long incarceration in hospital the pleasure of being free to roam where I liked and do what I liked was sufficient to fill my days. I didn't need people as well.

Under the spell of the river and the deep shrubbery that led to it I became Sir Henry Principality, a Royalist gentleman of my own invention, and when Sir Henry came upon a long low wooden hut half-concealed by the sweeping arms of a wych elm he knew instinctively that he had stumbled upon Cromwell's local headquarters. He crept closer and listened for the sound of voices. There was only the rustle of leaves and the murmur of a wood pigeon. With sword unsheathed he flung open the door and strode boldly within.

Clad in a paint-smeared artist's smock my grandmother looked up mildly and said: 'I'm marbling paper.'

Sir Henry faded like a shadow on the wall. I went over to the big worktable and peered into the oily swirl of colours in the galvanised bath. Sheets of decorated paper were spread out to dry.

'Is this one of your hobbies, Granny?'

'Yes.'

'Can I try it?'

'Yes, if you wish.'

She showed me how to lay the paper down feather-lightly on the surface of the oil paint, but although I followed her directions with the utmost care the result was nothing like hers; instead of an airy pirouette of blue on green, mine was a series of uncouth blotches. I asked if I could try again, but the result was no better.

'I daresay your talents lie in other directions,' she said courteously and stood waiting while I took my time gazing round the big sun-dappled hut that smelled of turps and dust and coconut matting.

The whole place was crammed with the evidence of her hobbies; easels holding half-completed paintings, a music stand containing an open score and a loom threaded with what looked like a length of carpet. A silver flute lay beside an almost completed jigsaw puzzle and then, sitting on a large copy of Turnbull's *Atlas of the British Empire* with her limbs tucked tidily beneath her body was Katinka. She was watching me.

'I wish I had a place like this at home,' I said.

'Your grandfather had it built for me so that I shouldn't make a mess in the house and annoy the servants.'

'Does Mrs Penney ever get annoyed?'

'Only in a case of wilful thoughtlessness.'

I made a note that this was a misdemeanour to be avoided at all costs then my gaze returned to the flute. 'Is that one of the things they play sideways?'

'Yes.'

'Can you show me?'

My grandmother picked up the flute, worked her brown lips a little and then prepared a small hole between them. A sparkle of sound rose and fell in the still summer air; warm bubbling blackbird notes, clear high notes stripped cold and pure as a glacier, all of them combining in a fragment of lilting, happy-sad waltz.

'Oh, play some more! *Please* . . .'

But she smiled and laid the flute back on the table. Her speckled fingers toyed with the floppy bow at the neck of her smock and I suddenly realised that she was waiting for me to leave. That although she liked me in the same way that I liked her, she was

23

nevertheless waiting for the moment when she would be left to her own devices.

'I expect it will soon be time for tea.'

'Are you coming too?'

'No, I shall come a little later.'

Katinka stood up and arched her spine before stepping off the *Atlas*. Picking a delicate pathway across the littered table she jumped down onto the floor.

'I think she would like to go with you,' my grandmother said. 'Mrs Penney normally gives her some milk in the kitchen at four o'clock.'

So Katinka and I crossed the lawn side by side, she with tail held high and ears pricked as if she could already hear the clink of the saucer. I escorted her to the kitchen and found a strange young woman sitting in Mrs Penney's basket chair with a baby on her lap.

'This is my daughter Edith, Miss,' Mrs Penney said. 'She always comes round on a Thursday.'

Edith was a red-faced girl with shingled hair and big teeth bared in a slightly daft smile. I shook hands with her while Mrs Penney refilled their teacups and then poured some milk for Katinka.

'Want to hold him, do you?' Edith folded the baby's shawl a little more tightly round its body before proffering it. Surprised and oddly embarrassed, I took it and held it awkwardly on outstretched forearms.

Edith giggled. 'Oh my, you do look funny! Ain't you ever held a baby before?'

I confessed that I hadn't. That until today I'd never even seen one close to.

'Well, hold him up against you,' her giggles increased. 'Go on, he won't bite!'

Gingerly I did as she advised, and stood to attention with the baby shouldered like a small dumpy musket. It began to squirm, and to make little whickering noises that filled me with awe. It struck me for the first time that it was really alive.

'What's its name?'

'Willie, like his dad. Rock him about a bit, he likes that.'

I did so, and the baby's head flopped drunkenly against my neck. I began to enjoy the feel of its soft warmth, the stirrings of its limbs

24

muffled beneath the shawl. I wanted to look at them.

'Seen his little feet, have you, Miss?' Mrs Penney might have guessed. 'Ever so wee they are.'

I sat down and carefully peeled away layers of shawl, flannelette and rabbit wool. Its legs were bent at the knee, bringing the tiny pinky-blue feet soles-together.

'It's lovely,' I said.

'*Him*,' Mrs Penney and her daughter laughed in unison. 'It's a *him!*'

And believe it or not, I didn't want to give it back. I had never played with dolls, but the strangeness of the warm living creature had touched some deeply buried little growth point in me and I wanted to keep it, to hug it to me, to undress and dress it, to play mothers-and-fathers with it. It squinnied up at me, its bald head unexpectedly heavy against my bare arm.

'Aah, he likes her! – '

'Oh look, Miss, he's smiling at you . . .' I had never seen Mrs Penney so animated. Her face was flushed and damp with a sort of love that excited and tantalised me. I returned Willie to his mother with reluctance.

And perhaps everything might have been different if Katinka hadn't decided to make friends with me that evening. I was eating supper alone in the dining-room and instead of going to her usual chair by the window she paused by my side and then leaped grace- fully onto the bit of lap that wasn't under the table. Hastily I made room for her, and after a cursory inspection of my plate she settled down and began to purr.

'Dear little baby,' I said, tickling her ears, and at that moment a new game began that was far better than anything Sir Henry Princi- pality had to offer.

It began simply enough; no more than picking Katinka up in my arms and rocking her to and fro. She seemed to enjoy it for she offered no resistance, and I quickly became familiar with the warm softness of her body. It had the same strange appeal as Willie's, and with familiarity came a deep yearning to look after her. To minister to all her needs, to protect and enfold her.

Without mentioning Edith's baby I asked my grandmother

whether I could groom Katinka's coat and she said how very thoughtful and gave me a small whalebone hairbrush. I brushed her night and morning and once took her up to the bathroom and washed her paws in warm water and lavender toilet soap. For some reason this experience filled her with great alarm and she shot out of my arms and made for the door, which luckily was closed. I caught her again, but her very obvious fear of the water released a great gush of maternal tenderness in me and I rocked her to and fro and said that she only need have her paws washed if she got them especially dirty and then put them in her mouth.

I had placed her in the wickerwork basinette and was pushing her slowly along the upper landing when Mrs Penney suddenly appeared. Up until that moment Katinka had seemed to be enjoying the experience, but on hearing Mrs Penney's voice she leaped from under the hood and fled downstairs.

'Playing babies, were you, Miss?' Mrs Penney seemed not to notice my embarrassment. 'Well now, we'll have to see what we can do, won't we?'

I didn't know what she meant, and endured a couple of troubled hours in case she told my grandmother and the game was forbidden because of the strange secret pleasure it gave me. But when I went up to my room I found a pile of dolls' clothes on the counterpane and knew instantly that she had put them there. Embroidered dresses and petticoats, lacy matinée jackets and some tiny white kid boots with real little laces.

It took some while to persuade Katinka in to one of the dresses, but once her arms were through the sleeves and the bodice was buttoned down her back there was nothing she could do. I suppose she must have looked very funny, but I know I didn't think so. The game was too real and too serious for that, and so Katinka wore straw bonnets and camisoles with lace insertion and frilly drawers with a hole cut in to accommodate her tail. I tried very hard to make her wear the white kid boots, but however firmly I laced them she was able to get rid of them with a strong flick of the back legs.

I also found a means of harnessing her into the basinette, and Mrs Penney (and Edith, when she was there on the following Thursday), laughed and clapped their hands to see a cat dressed up in dolls' clothes. They said that it would make a comical picture postcard. I believe that my grandmother remained in ignorance of Katinka's metamorphosis from cat into human infant; if she was aware of it, she made no comment.

The day the game died was the day I received a letter from my father enclosing a copy of *Treasure Island*. I had never read the book before, and gorged myself on it for a whole day lying down by the river where dragonflies skimmed and moorhens went stealthily about their business. Katinka remained unbrushed, undressed, and I fell asleep when the last page had been turned that night, secure in the knowledge that babies were stupid and that once again the only decent thing to be was a boy.

I became Jim Hawkins of course, and Katinka, not well adapted for the role of Long John Silver, became Ben Gunn. She didn't seem to understand that she had gone off her head with loneliness on the island and once or twice I had to get quite cross with her. Yet that game, like all the others I played at Riverside Lodge during my convalescence, had a vigour, a marvellous sun-filled magic that I was never able to recapture.

Late spring deepened into a summer passionate with paeonies and roses and then bowlfuls of strawberries. Mr Horringer, who worked in the garden, left off his celluloid collar and took to a panama hat. Whenever I encountered my grandmother she would make a little courteous conversation and then she would be gone again, a small long-skirted figure gliding up to her bedroom (a sanctum I had not been invited to enter), or across the lawn to her garden hut. Sometimes after I had gone to bed I would hear the sound of her flute weaving an eerie saraband; I was glad that she didn't intrude too heavily into my private world and I think that she felt the same way about me. In other words, we were compatible.

I returned to being Sir Henry Principality for a while, and then quite abruptly everything changed. One minute I was the centre of my own universe, and the next it had all disappeared. As if I had just opened my eyes for the first time I suddenly became aware of the sheer prodigious reality of another person: and that person was Katinka.

No longer a make-believe wolfhound with a message in secret ink tied round her neck, I saw her for the very first time as she really was, and as she had always really been, if only I had had the sense to see; a small silver-and-black animal of matchless grace and enchantment sitting in a patch of apricot sunlight removing a speck of dirt from its back toes.

I untied the message from round her neck and threw it away, and too overcome by humility even to stroke her, told her that from now on we would only ever play the kind of games she wanted to play.

As I say, it all began with the recognition of her beauty. I saw for the first time that cats are constructed almost entirely of curves; the easy curve of the spine, the rounded shape of the haunches, the neat little nut-shaped skull and the gentle swell of the breast. Even her whiskers curved in a downward sweep to meet the upward tilt of her lips. The only straight thing was her nose; seven-eighths of an inch of dark grey plush. I remember measuring it with Mrs Penney's tape measure.

And my whole life seemed to dissolve in the joy of watching her. I couldn't sleep for thinking about her, and began to realise that it was cruel to expect her to spend the long nights down in the kitchen all by herself. Huddled in her lonely basket by the black iron range she would be longing for my company as much as I longed for hers. So I crept downstairs and brought her back to my room, still warm with sleep and quite passive after the first little chirrup of surprise.

She slept folded against my shoulder under the bedcovers and I listened to the easy rhythm of her purrs gradually fading into an irregular little popping sound as she relaxed in slumber. We did this every night, and awakened by her yawnings and rustlings at first light I would dress hurriedly and creep with her out into the pearl-coloured garden. Katinka would stand with ears pricked and nostrils raised as if testing the flavour of the new day, then make for one of the flowerbeds. After a careful reconnaissance she would dig a small latrine over which she would perch herself, and remain for a few moments rapt as a visionary while I hovered politely nearby.

This first duty completed she would fill the time before breakfast with apparently aimless wandering round the garden, pausing every now and then to sniff at a plant and occasionally freezing into sudden immobility as if struck by a powerful thought. Sometimes the need to immerse myself in her life entailed crawling through very small holes in hedges, and once I climbed out of a boxroom window in order to join her on the flat scullery roof.

I discovered that her life, now freed from my interference, was divided between sleeping, grooming, strolling and watching things. It was a life of sublime neatness, each small task being performed with grace, competence and economy, and when I talked to her she would sometimes stare into my face with her cool green eyes as if she saw right into my mind. But I could never really see into hers. I seemed to get so far, then the dense black of her pupils would baffle all attempt at interpretation and I would remember being told that there is a blankness in animals' eyes because they have no souls. I loved the idea of Katinka having no soul because it made her seem so clean and uncluttered.

Although I remained true to my vow not to make her play my sort of games any more, I worked very hard at trying to make life easier and pleasanter for her; lifting her down from chairs to save her the bother of jumping; stealing little tidbits from the kitchen , and once bringing her a dead sparrow wrapped in my handkerchief. (She sniffed it diplomatically before turning her attention elsewhere.)

I discovered that she liked to chase a piece of paper rolled into a ball. Evenings after supper seemed to be her favourite time for this, and so I would carry her – to save her the fag of walking – from her chair in the dining room and out onto the big lawn and bowl a gentle underarm for her. And she would crouch, tense as a coiled spring, with her eyes changing from limpid green to a round and fearsome black. She would leap after the ball, bat at it with her paws, seize it and roll over with it held in extended claws like wicked little fingers. Sometimes she would chase it for quite a long while on her own, crouching, springing, and flicking it high in the air, and I would wait with humble adoration for the moment when she wanted me to throw it again.

'The savage that lurks beneath the soft fur,' my grandmother said, pausing to watch one evening.

'She's jolly good at catching.'

'Of course she is. That is her job.'

Despite the many roles I had previously inflicted upon her, I had never thought of Katinka as someone having a job, like Mrs Penney or Mr Horringer.

'She is here to catch the rats and mice,' my grandmother said with a brown-lipped smile. Then turned her attention to me. 'I believe your father will see a great change in you for the better when he comes to fetch you on Saturday.'

'This Saturday?' My heart slumped.

She nodded, her large faded eyes filled with kindness. 'He will be arriving in time for tea and Mrs Penney has promised to make a chocolate cake. Even as a small boy, chocolate cake was always his favourite.'

She moved away in the direction of her garden hut, and I was left with the realisation that even magic is ephemeral.

Katinka had stopped playing ball and was sitting in the privacy of an acanthus, performing her toilet. With one back leg raised stiffly against her shoulder while she washed her intimate parts she looked like someone playing a 'cello. I told her that I would be going away in two days' time and she looked up as if she understood and was sad.

I sat down close to her, and however hard I clenched my hands and gritted my teeth I couldn't stop the precious minutes from slipping past. All I could do, as she completed her ablutions, was to vow that from this moment onward I would make the very most of her company. That every waking and sleeping second should be spent in her presence in order that I might amass a great storehouse of memories to see me through the barren years ahead.

'Katinka follows the child everywhere,' I heard my grandmother say to Mrs Penney. 'She is like her shadow.'

But a close observer, (or at least, one with fewer hobbies), would have recognised that it was the other way around. That it was I who was following Katinka. Occasionally she disappeared from sight and much anguished searching would disclose her curled snake-like in a patch of long grass almost as if she were hiding from me. So I would sit beside her, murmuring a litany of love and tracing the sweet silver tabby markings on her forehead with my finger. I didn't know then about the ancient Egyptians worshipping cats, but if I had I would not only have found the idea totally feasible, I would have joined the club. In fact, I already did worship Katinka; I worshipped her to the extent of subjugating my own wavering personality completely, and although I still loved my father I didn't want to live with him at home any more. I only wanted to live at Riverside Lodge, with everything exactly the way it was now.

The chocolate cake was made and my clean frock was hanging over the back of my bedroom chair.

'Now go and wash your hands and face and brush your hair, Miss, because your Daddy will be here soon,' Mrs Penney said.

With a heavy heart and dragging feet I went, carrying Katinka with me. She sat on the bed while I changed my frock. My suitcase had already been packed except for my sponge bag.

'There's not much longer now,' I told her. 'Only about two hours.'

And she looked so beautiful that I sat down beside her, and instead of brushing my hair began to brush her instead. It was the first time I had done so since playing babies with her, and I watched her spine quiver pleasurably beneath the long strokes sweeping her from head to tail. Purring, she stood up and butted my hand with her forehead. In an agony of love I picked her up and cradled her in my arms, holding her upside-down while I kissed her little black pads and then bent low to rub my cheek against hers. The sound of her purring increased, and mingled with the soft chug of a motor car coming up the drive. I reached for the hairbrush again and began to sweep it down the soft silver-grey of her belly. The motor's engine stopped, I heard the clunk of its door and then footsteps crunching on the gravel. My father's voice called hullo.

I resolved not to go down. To stay where I was, to run away and hide if need be. I brushed Katinka's belly harder, unaware that, like the motor car's engine, her purring had also stopped. And then it happened.

With a sudden wild lunge that knocked the hairbrush flying Katinka sprang upright in my lap and lashed out. Her claws missed my face and ripped deep into the side of my neck and as the pain seared I glimpsed, just for an instant, the depth of murderous pent-up hatred in her eyes.

Too shocked to move or to cry out I crouched on the side of the bed with my hands round my neck, and when I took them away they were streaked with blood and I was like poor Beryl who had died after being slit open in the isolation hospital.

I couldn't seem to do anything; couldn't even cry. Katinka's action appeared to have terminated all feeling and I saw her trip lightly

31

downstairs as I crept to the bathroom to bathe the wounds.

I heard my name called as I dabbed at the two long scratches and at the series of peppered holes still welling blood. I called back that I was coming, but in a voice that they wouldn't have heard. I went on dabbing until the blood stopped then turned up the collar of my frock, smoothed my hair and walked downstairs.

I found them in the drawing-room, bathed in a mellow afternoon light. My father held out his arms when he saw me.

'Hullo, Tup!' That was my nickname. Short for Tuppence.

'Hullo.'

'My heavens, you do look well! All nice and brown, and you've grown tremendously.'

'I grew in hospital,' I said. 'Before I came here.'

I stood looking up into his brown eyes. He had a small moustache that was lighter in colour than his hair. He put his hands on my shoulders and carefully smoothed my collar down flat. I backed away, but managed to smile.

We had tea. Pale China tea in shallow cups, cucumber sandwiches with the crusts cut off, and scones like little fluted castles. My grandmother, presiding, also steered the conversation. We spoke of the weather, of the level to which the river had dropped, of the Kellogg Pact for the abolition of all future wars and of Mr Thomas Hardy the author being very ill.

Accepting a second cup of tea my father turned to me and asked whether I had made any special friends at Riverside Lodge.

'No,' I sat with my hand guarding my neck. 'No, not really.'

We got to the chocolate cake, richly iced and decorated with sugared violets, but I couldn't eat any. Sitting opposite me on a beaded Victorian chair was Katinka with her limbs tucked beneath her body and her head bowed as if in prayer. My eyes were stone-dry but I couldn't look at her. I still couldn't seem to do anything the way I did normally.

I heard my grandmother speak my name, and looked up unwillingly to meet her pale tobacco-coloured eyes.

'As you and Katinka are so fond of one another, would you like to take her home with you?'

My eyes filled, then. Blinking furiously I managed to say No thank you.

32

'Oh . . .' She sounded mildly surprised. 'I have already asked your father's permission, and he has given it.'

'No, thank you.'

I wanted to add that I didn't like cats very much, but the words wouldn't come. In any case, it wasn't true. Not even now.

So she changed the subject, and shortly afterwards my suitcase was placed on the dickey seat and I climbed up into the bull-nosed Morris beside my father. My grandmother and Mrs Penney stood waving goodbye but Katinka wasn't there.

The tears had started before we reached the end of the drive and they rolled down my cheeks and splashed into my lap. I cried very quietly and my father asked no questions, offered no useless comfort; just let me soak his big white handkerchief with all the bitterness of my grief. He was a nice man, my father.

STRAUSS

Mark Ronson

With a sigh of relief Isobel glimpsed a half-hidden signpost when she braked at the T-junction. She could just make out the name 'Spadeadam' on its right-hand arm, and gratefully she turned her small Nippon-Leyland on to the road which inclined to the north. With luck she still might be in time for the interview with her new boss.

It had been a wearying drive up from London and once she left the motorway and entered the wide, wild Border country she took a wrong turning and lost herself in narrow lanes which seemed to meander to nowhere. Unfortunately her map was not detailed enough to include such minor roads, although her destination was outlined in red with large capitals warning DANGER ZONE. A large area of land once picturesquely (and accurately, Isobel was to discover) known as Spade Adam Waste, it was a no-go area belonging to the Ministry of Defence. Blue Streak rocket motors had been tested here but when Britain's space ambitions were abandoned it became the scene of less spectacular but more secret research.

As the car climbed out of the Irthing Valley, Isobel looked down at the scattered village of Gilsland. Afternoon smoke pencilled from its chimneys, and she wondered in which of the homes she would be accommodated. Glancing at her watch again, she unconsciously pressed the accelerator pedal. In his rather formal letter Dr Swan had written that he would expect her at sixteen hours. It would seem so *ineffectual* if she arrived late with a story about getting lost.

At the moment she was too tense to appreciate the Cumbrian landscape spread out below her, but she already sensed that here she would find tranquillity after her life in the capital. And in these days of cutbacks and redundancy, she was lucky to have got such a post.

Suddenly the car rattled over a cattle grid. Signs warned innocent motorists to go no further, and a minute later she pulled up in front of a massive barber's pole blocking the road.

A Ministry of Defence policeman emerged from his white hut and looked at her inquiringly.

'I have an appointment with Dr Swan,' she said, winding down the window and relishing the bite of the autumnal air. 'I'm . . .'

'Grantham, Isobel,' he said, proffering his clipboard. 'Sign in, please, Miss.'

As she wrote her name neatly he observed her with interest. Any addition to the local talent was welcome, and her long fair hair was rather attractive though it was in contrast to the rest of her appearance which he thought of as 'schoolmarmish'. But he decided he'd risk inviting her for a drink at the Samson in a couple of days. Some of these quiet ones . . .

'Right,' he said, retrieving his board. 'Take the road marked R-1. The doctor's unit is about a mile through the pines, and if you see a bloody great tank coming towards you pull over. Things are getting pretty busy here since the Cold War has started to freeze again.'

'Yes,' said Isobel. 'It's all rather worrying – and the war in the Middle East seems to be getting worse.'

'Roll on, Armageddon,' the guard said cheerfully.

Isobel followed the signs through an artificial forest, driving as fast as she dared and nervous at every bend that she would find herself face-to-face with some clanking steel monster. But she saw nothing apart from a wild deer and she was only five minutes late when she halted in a car park in front of a large concrete building which reminded her of a wartime bunker. Its drabness was only relieved by a red sign which stated 'Radiation Research Unit – Positively No Unauthorized Personnel'. Beneath it some humorist had scrawled, 'All hope abandon, ye who enter here.'

Dr Swan looked up from his orderly desk at his new technical assistant. He had expected her to be older, and without her glasses she would be rather good-looking, especially with that long soft hair. She would certainly be an improvement on the retired and un-lamented Davidson. Perhaps it wouldn't be so bad having a girl to do the job after all! He stood up – not sure whether she would be pleased or offended by the gesture.

Isobel saw a youngish man with receding hair rise awkwardly from behind his desk. She had expected him to be older – more of a professor – and she almost blushed when he shook her hand and said, 'Welcome to our little establishment. Would you like some tea after your long drive?'

'If it's no bother.'

'Sugar?'

'No, thank you.'

'Good. Biscuits?'

'If it's no bother.'

'No bother, I'm sure.'

There was a long pause.

'So you were at Crystal Palace. Some interesting work going on there . . .'

'Yes. I was on canines in the genetic engineering lab . . .'

'It's cats here.'

'Oh good, I love cats . . .'

How stupid she was! The words had popped out before she could stop herself. As a good lab technician she was not supposed to have an emotional interest in her charges. Sentimental people were suspect in case they suddenly became conscience-stricken and provided propaganda material for animal defence groups.

Then – miraculously it seemed – Dr Swan smiled and said, 'So do I. My mother breeds Burmese.'

The tea tray was carried in by an orderly wearing army uniform. Seeing Isobel's look of surprise, Dr Swan said, 'Here we have round-the-clock military security and, as we are some distance from the main complex, we have an army canteen attached. You'll soon get used to the precautions and the isolation – at least we are not likely to be troubled by protesters. This place is one of the best kept secrets since Pearl Harbour . . .' He laughed. 'That's why you were so positively vetted.'

'I still have no idea of what happens here.'

'Neither had I until I was actually transferred from Harwell,' said Dr Swan, offering her the chocolate biscuits. 'Its an experiment which has been going on for some years – started back in 1983 actually. I've been here for five years, and I still feel there is a

36

science fiction element about it.'

He gave her a slight smile, knowing that he hardly sounded like a seasoned project leader, a scientist at the top of his rarified discipline.

'If you're not too tired I'll give you a very brief outline of what is being attempted, and then you can slip off and settle into Mrs Barwick's in the village. Tomorrow you can see the radiation chamber and start getting an idea of the routine.'

She inclined her head in a way which he thought was rather attractive and, putting the tips of his fingers together, he began his lecture on what he hoped would be a light note.

'I don't know if you are acquainted with Scottish mythology, Miss Grantham, but what we are doing here is code-named Operation Taghairn. Some Celt at the Military must have a whimsical mind.

'Taghairn was a rather unpleasant magical rite performed in Scotland in medieval times and, indeed, later. I believe it was last recorded at the beginning of the seventeenth century. It consisted of roasting a succession of live cats on a spit until their suffering induced a Master Cat to appear and grant a wish in return for the ritual being stopped.'

'You mean – we're roasting cats?' exclaimed Isobel.

Dr Swan laughed. On a jotter he drew a cat out of a large O and three small ones, adding an S for the tail. The project seemed so implausible that he always had difficulty in describing it.

'We are not cooking cats, but we are in search of a very big boon,' he continued. 'Back in 1982 two things happened which led to the setting up of this project. The first came about when a German scientist investigated the undersea craters off the island of Vulcano in the Mediterranean. Volcanic gases issuing from these craters heated the surrounding water to over a hundred degrees. And it was in these conditions that Dr Setter, of Regensburg University, discovered bacterium capable of thriving at temperatures of 105°C.

'Not only did these organisms live in heat hitherto thought impossible for any form of life, but oxygen was not available – indeed, it was found to be lethal to them.

'A result of the discovery was that many biologists took the view that what had been considered the environment necessary to sustain life should be reappraised, that we must get away from the idea that all life forms require what is essential for *us*. Goodness knows what living organisms may be drifting in the ultimate cold of space . . .'

Isobel noted how Dr Swan's face became animated as he warmed to his subject.

'The second thing was that the government of the day came to the conclusion that nuclear war – with its subsequent universal annihilation of life as we know it – was inevitable. Oh, perhaps not in our lifetimes, but sooner or later the buttons would be pressed. So, inspired by the new biological thinking, it was decided to investigate the possibility of engineering living material to withstand the radiation which could be expected following a nuclear strike.

'The plan was to expose succeeding generations of subjects to increasing radio-active dosage.

'To begin with several species of higher mammals were used. Monkeys proved to be very disappointing. Stress was their weak point and they died for psychological reasons rather than physical ones. And the dogs – well, dogs don't have nine lives like cats.'

Pleased with his little joke, Dr Swan missed Isobel's ironic tone when she said, 'So instead of roasting cats, we have been irradiating them.'

'Precisely. The dosage was imperceptibly increased with each generation and genetic immunity grew. As one would expect there was a high abortion and mutation rate, but despite that we have now achieved two perfect breeding specimens capable of absorbing radiation which would be completely lethal to a normal animal.'

'You mean that these generations of cats have never left the radiation chamber.'

'Correct. We could not take them out because they are dangerously radio-active.' He laughed. 'There is a piece of folklore here that when the lights are switched off for their sleeping period they glow slightly.'

'Then what monstrosities have you got in there?' Isobel asked.

'A pair of nice, normal-looking pussy cats. All mutations were weeded out. But you must see the significance of what has been achieved. It is the first step to creating a breed of humans capable of withstanding radiation which could mean that atomic warfare would not necessarily bring about the extinction of mankind.'

'I see what you meant when you said "science fiction"!'

'We're still a very long way from that goal. And with the way things are going in Europe and the Middle East, I wonder whether there'll be time. Thank goodness I'm a simple scientist, cats are my concern not politics.'

'Now I understand the security and why I was so thoroughly investigated.'

'You can imagine the effect if news of our work leaked out. Not that it would come as a shock to the Russians – I believe they're carrying out a similar programme with aquatic life – but with our own people. Remember the demands for a moratorium on genetic engineering? And imagine if the Animal Freedom League tried to liberate Strauss and Tiggy!'

He winced at the thought.

'But that's enough for today. If you'd like to follow my station waggon, I'll lead you to Mrs Barwick's.'

Next morning Isobel saw her charges. Dr Swan was already waiting for her when she arrived. He led her down a long corridor to a special 'safety' room where they donned protective overalls.

'We won't be entering the chamber today,' he explained. 'We have to dress up like spacemen for that. Normally robotic equipment takes care of feeding and the removal of litter which has to be sealed in lead containers for disposal at Windscale. Each animal has an implanted micro-transmitter which enables us to monitor their vital functions.'

He pressed a control button and a heavy, lead-shielded door slid open with a hiss of compressed air.

'Behold our little family.'

Isobel found herself in a long fluorescent bright laboratory lined with electronic equipment and television screens on which flashed numeric displays. From a computer printer an endless strip of paper folded itself into a wire basket.

Dr Swan held it up and began to examine the wavy lines which had been penned on it, representing the life rhythms of the two animals at the far end of the room.

'Go on, take a look at them while I check this,' he said.

As Isobel walked towards the radiation-proof glass wall, she wondered apprehensively what she would see – what travesties would she be expected to devote her working life to?

She almost laughed with relief at what she saw.

Beyond the leaded glass was a large chamber containing a scratching pole, an old tartan rug, a disreputable teddy bear and two cats. A beautiful Siamese seal point regarded her with blue-eyed curiosity while in the background his mate, a grey tabby, lay indolently on the rug. It was obvious that she would soon be a mother.

'You must be Strauss,' Isobel said to the Siamese as he rose on his slender legs and moved gracefully towards her, expressing his friendliness by rubbing against the glass. Isobel found herself responding by stroking her side of the barrier.

'Isn't he a lovely fellow?' said Dr Swan.

'Why is he called Strauss?'

'Naming male cats after composers was an idiosyncrasy of our first director. The original animal to be irradiated was Mozart, and his surviving son was Beethoven and so on.'

'And the other?'

'Tiggy. Short for Mrs Tiggy-Winkle. All females were called after Beatrix Potter characters.'

Fascinated by Isobel's gloved fingers, Strauss reared on his hind legs and attempted to touch them with his chocolate paws. From a loudspeaker came his frustrated yowl and for the first time Isobel had doubts about her work. She tried to imagine generations of these animals locked in this small poisoned world. It was not as if she could see any benefit for mankind from the programme – her justification for experiments on animals. Who cared if life was to continue after a nuclear holocaust? What sort of life – and in what sort of world?

Beside her Dr Swan glanced at a large studio clock.

'Watch,' he said. 'They always know.'

Tiggy suddenly climbed to her feet and her cracked mew sounded from the speaker. Strauss turned from the window and joined her pacing excitedly before a panel in the wall.

The panel slid back and a tray appeared on which was a bowl of milk and two dishes of food. The cats leapt forward and began to devour it, Strauss growling slightly when Tiggy placed a warning paw on his head to keep him away from her dish.

'Come, I'll show you the rest of the labs,' said Dr Swan, turning away.

As they left the long room the rasping sound of Tiggy lapping milk was amplified over the speakers, and Isobel felt herself give a slight shudder.

On Isobel's second Sunday at the laboratory Dr Swan asked if she would care to spend her free afternoon with him, he'd like to show her some of the local countryside. It was an invitation which she hoped that she did not appear too eager to accept. And then she thought: I'm not going to be hypocritical and I don't want to play games. I like Dr Swan a lot, so why try to hide it.

He was pleased at her ready acceptance. Over the past few days they had been drawn together, not only by the excitement of Tiggy's forthcoming confinement but by the realization that they shared a lot in common. Both were shy, yet each felt that here at last was someone with whom they could communicate.

After lunch they drove the few miles to Gelt Woods – a favourite beauty spot of his – and soon they were strolling on a carpet of sere leaves beside a stream murmuring between banks of ferns and outcrops of reddish rock. And it seemed the most natural thing when their hands came into accidental contact for him to take firm hold of her fingers.

Their talk was trivial . . . anecdotes about past work and present colleagues, and inevitably their childhood and the discovery that both had suffered by being only children.

They sat on a log by the rippling water. Shafts of pale sunlight rained on them through the network of branches above, and somewhere an unidentified bird trilled as though nature had nothing to fear from the modern world.

Suddenly Isobel turned and faced Dr Swan who held both her hands.

'I have a confession I feel I must make,' she said.

Oh no, he thought. She's going to tell me she's married!

'I have always tried to be detached from my work,' she continued. 'Although I'm fond of animals, I've never found it difficult to keep a scientific attitude to laboratory subjects.'

'But?'

'It's . . . it's Strauss and Tiggy. I have begun to feel that what has been done to them is obscene – yes, obscene! I mean, they're

41

condemned to live for ever in a room full of pure poison, and what worries me – and I must say this – is that it does not strike you in the same way.'

She pulled her hands away and looked at him defiantly.

Carefully choosing his words, he said, 'I think I can understand what you are saying. We wouldn't be human if at times we did not feel emotional about things which are important to us. This is a new environment and you have obviously found this experiment very startling . . .'

And I have found myself capable of feelings which I had not thought possible, she added mentally.

'But the cats are not suffering. Their ancestors probably did, but there is nothing we can do about that now. I should be very distressed if you saw me as a . . . if you felt I was uncaring . . .'

'It was when I went into the chamber for the first time in my anti-radiation suit and helmet. After I'd examined Tiggy, Strauss came and jumped onto my lap and when I went to stroke him I could not feel his fur because of my gauntlets.'

'But surely it's something more than that which is upsetting you,' said Dr Swan gently. 'After all, you are used to laboratory conditions.'

'But not these. It's like that horrible magical ceremony you told me about . . . but you are right. Holding Strauss and yet not being able to feel him seemed to reflect my life. I – I see life all around me, and yet it's as though I've never been able to grasp it somehow. Oh, you must think I'm mad.'

'Not at all.' He carefully removed her glasses and a moment later his arms were round her.

'I do know what you mean,' he said. 'I have made the laboratory, and a succession of cats with musical names, my world while the real world . . . real life has been going on outside the perimeter of Spadeadam. But now . . .'

He did not say any more but kissed her while nearby the bird sang triumphantly.

It was a very different couple who drove back to Gilsland late that afternoon. Even when the announcer interrupted the music programme coming softly over the car radio with the grave news that Russian tanks were massing on the East German border, his words did nothing to take away Isobel's smile of inner happiness.

When Isobel halted at the checkpoint on Monday morning she saw that the MOD policeman had a holstered revolver strapped over his dark blue uniform.

'We're on Security Red,' he explained almost apologetically. 'Bloody Russians! What can they gain from all this?'

She shrugged and took back her identity card.

Normally she took an interest in international affairs, believing it was correct that every citizen did so, but today the focus of her attention had narrowed to a fine point. It centred only on herself and her new found emotions. She also felt rather breathless, wondering what it would be like to see him again after those wonderful moments in Gelt Woods.

She had to pull over while a convoy of tanks, with their secret radar aerials revolving, slithered past on their steel tracks. It meant nothing to her that a canteen rumour said that they were going to be rushed to Germany across the North Sea.

She parked as usual and went to the monitoring room to begin the day's work, correlating information which various electronic monitors provided by a never-ending surveillance of the cats.

'I think Tiggy is due to produce any minute now,' said a technician who had just completed the night shift. 'Her pulse and respiration are increasing, and Strauss is unusually restless.'

'Thank you,' said Isobel. 'This may be the great day.'

Dr Swan's voice interrupted from the PA system.

'Miss Grantham, will you please report to my office immediately.'

He sounded so crisp and formal that the young technician gave Isobel a sympathetic grin.

'Good luck,' he said. 'You'd think it was him that was going to have kittens, he's been that jumpy lately.'

Isobel put down her clipboard and hurried to the director's office.

'Come in,' came the still formal voice when she tapped on the door. But as soon as it shut behind her Dr Swan swept her into his embrace. She clung to him in a surge of delight at the discovery that yesterday had not been some curious day dream.

'David,' she said.

They were finally interrupted by a knock, a knock which made

43

them spring apart guiltily.

'Sir, I think you should suit up,' said a laboratory assistant. 'Tiggy's going into labour.'

A few minutes later Dr Swan and Isobel, dressed like spacemen, entered the shielded airlock leading into the cats' chamber. The isotopes which normally kept it in a constant state of radio-activity had been retracted into lead containers, but even so they had to breathe air carried in cylinders.

They found Tiggy lying on her side, her chest heaving. Strauss was circling her, his crazy blue eyes fixed on her while his distinctive yowl echoed in Isobel's earphones.

Dr Swan pointed at him and she understood. She picked up the coffee and chocolate animal while her new lover bent over Tiggy.

'It's all right, Strauss,' she said soothingly, although it was doubtful if he could hear through her radiation-proof plastiquartz.

On her rug Tiggy appeared to go into a convulsion. Dr Swan held her back, and then with remarkable rapidity her white blind kittens appeared.

'They seem to be all right,' he said over the radio link. 'For the first time we have had a litter without mutations. It means that at last the experiment has succeeded.'

Isobel knelt beside him, gazing at the four tiny creatures already nudging their mother's belly. Before she could stop him Strauss leapt from her arms. She feared he might injure them, but he merely joined his mate in cleaning their brood.

They left the chamber as flashing lights warned that radiation levels were returning to their normal intensity. Once through the anti-contamination sprays, they joined their colleagues in front of the chamber window. Champagne corks popped and toasts were drunk to the new family. The wine seemed to bubble in Isobel's blood as she watched Strauss gently prod a kitten with an inquisitive paw, and then noticed the look of exultation on Dr Swan's face reflected in the glass.

The celebration only sobered when someone switched on a transistor radio for the Prime Minister's broadcast to the nation.

For Isobel the passing days were a secret delight – secret because she and David Swan did their best to keep their love affair private, not realizing the change in them both was so obvious that it was the talk of the canteen. The passion of these two unlikely people, coupled with the progress of the kittens, provided a comforting conversational topic against the outside news which became daily more alarming.

Emergency sessions at the United Nations were followed by NATO declarations counter-blasted by the Warsaw Pact alliance. There were meetings at No 10 to which the leaders of the Tory and Labour opposition parties were invited. The *Financial Times* reported soaring prices for gold following the uprising in Estonia and the decision of France to declare herself a nuclear free zone.

And all the time Soviet armour rumbled into East Germany and an endless stream of USAF supertransports bridged the Atlantic. Yet at the Radiation Research Unit the progress of Chopin, Bartok, Mittens and Moppet remained the main interest, especially when their father's colouring began to appear through their white fur.

Isobel spent hours watching them through the window, recording their progress with a video camera. She was most intrigued by the attitude of Strauss. Often he attempted to play with one of his offspring, pawing it in the same way as he did his ball with the bell in it. Then Tiggy would hurry over – scribbles of light on a monitor indicating her concern – pick up the kitten by the scruff of the neck, and carry it to safety in the far corner.

'Poor Strauss,' Isobel would call and at her voice issuing from a loudspeaker he would rub himself against the glass.

Late one afternoon, after the kittens had developed enough to chase their father's chocolate tail, Dr Swan sat alone in the canteen waiting for Isobel. From the radio was a replay of the Prime Minister's speech to the House, claiming that if conventional conflict was to break out in Europe it did not necessarily mean an atomic war.

'In my heart I cannot believe that either of the great powers now confronting each other would resort to a nuclear strike even if non-nuclear weapons were employed,' came the carefully modulated voice. 'They know that it would only signal the automatic destruction of their own territory as well as those of their enemies.' And for once the Yah-boos of the Honourable Members were missing.

When Isobel entered Dr Swan saw with pleasure how she had

changed since she had first sat so primly in his study; now her face was animated and she wore a wispy vermilion scarf at her throat.

'Coffee?' he asked.

She shook her head.

'Sorry to be late. I was so busy videoing the brood's attempts at lapping milk I quite forgot the time. The fact that the radiation has been increased by a millicurie doesn't seem to have affected their spirits.'

'Let's get some fresh air,' he said. 'One can have too much of this hothouse atmosphere.'

Together they left the building, and he led her to a point which overlooked the whispering sea of conifers which covered much of Spadeadam. To the west the sun was low behind a dark bank of stratocumulus, its golden rays fanning above and below it and reminding Isobel of a scene from a holy picture.

Beyond the village of Gilsland fells rose to the distant Pennines. Surrounding hilltops were edged with the black lace of leafless trees.

An arrow formation of Fouga jets shrieked along the line of the Roman Wall and vanished, leaving their thunder rolling behind them. As it died Isobel suddenly had the curious sensation that she and David were the only people in the world.

'Isobel,' he began and turned her towards him – with the result that her eyes escaped the initial effect of the bomb. Yet, although she had closed her eyes expecting to be kissed, she saw the world turn white through her eyelids. She heard David scream and felt him sag in her arms. Radiation had melted his eyes and slime was running down his face. At the same time her body felt as though it had caught fire as the same radiation flowed through her.

Kneeling beside him on the pine needles, she saw an awesome glow above the Pennines and an incandescent cloud forming itself into the Hiroshima mushroom.

The strangest thing was that, apart from distant screams of those who had been looking south like Dr Swan, a great silence hung above them. Radiation travelled at the speed of light, but it would be several minutes before the blast wave from the warhead which had exploded above Birmingham reached them.

Aware that painful changes were taking place within her body, Isobel lay beside David and whispered, 'It'll be over soon, darling.'

From behind the hands which he pressed to his face she heard him mutter a single word.

'Strauss.'

'Yes,' said Isobel. 'Of course.'

Slowly she climbed to her feet and left her dying lover. She prayed that she could perform her duty before she collapsed. Behind her a vast pillar of flame marked the first strike but it meant nothing to her now. She had no doubt that British missiles were hurtling east, that the taxpayer was at last getting the benefit of the money which had been invested in them to keep the balance of power. But what did it matter? The world was dying second by second, and she felt a strange satisfaction that in a few minutes at the most she would make the final escape.

As she approached the research centre she saw the MOD policeman in the car park. He, too, had been blinded when the SS20 struck and now he staggered in a circle firing his revolver.

Isobel waited patiently until the gun was empty and then crossed to the building. She was just entering it when it seemed that all the colour was bleached out of the universe. To the north a rocket had successfully targeted on the nuclear submarine base at Holy Loch.

Inside she staggered down the corridor, oblivious to the blood trickling down her legs and leaving a trail on the mirror finish of the linoleum.

She pressed against the wall as a group of her colleagues, as yet untouched by radiation, came in a jostling pack towards her.

'Oh God, look at her skin,' a girl shouted. Then, in silence, they passed her, flattening themselves against the opposite wall as though she was something evil.

Alone again she made her way to the airlock and pressed the controls to open the great door. Warning chimes sounded, competing with the tape-recorded voice which was giving advice on what to do in the unlikely event of a nuclear attack.

The cats looked up at her inquisitively as she entered their chamber – never before had they seen an ordinary unprotected human in their domain. Strauss arched his back and then stood on his hindlegs, the claws of his forepaws hooked in the threads of her skirt.

Tiggy uncurled and stood beside him, her cracked voice expressing her pleasure while the kittens remained playing with their felt mouse.

'Strauss, you must come,' Isobel heard herself mutter through the waves of nausea which were now enfolding her. 'Come on, puss-puss . . .'

But the animals were reluctant to leave.

She tried to pick him up but he jumped back. Then she seized the kittens and walked through the airlock where batteries of warning lights were blinking in frenzy. The two cats followed, Strauss running his nose along the floor as scents from the outside world assailed him.

Afraid that she would not reach the main entrance down the seemingly endless corridor, she turned into a room where she knew there was an emergency door. Here she put her squirming burdens down and summoned her failing strength to turn the exit wheel. The door was ajar when the shockwave from the first bomb flattened the plantation like a reaping hook slicing through cornstalks. The south-facing wall of the building dissolved, and in the car park vehicles were rolled over and over.

From the PA system a tinny pre-recorded voice was almost drowned by the hurricane roar as it repeated, 'All personnel will proceed in an orderly fashion to their allotted assembly points . . . All personnel . . .' But there was no personnel left to obey.

The shriek of the hot wind died and silence returned while England to the south and Scotland to the north glowed eerily.

For a moment the cats sniffed the body of the dead girl. Then with his tail high, and Tiggy and the kittens following, Strauss stepped out to inherit his world.

Nine Lives

Stella Whitelaw

Lucinda Ward Barrington was an undeveloped cat lover. She had never owned a cat or lived with one, but she stopped to stroke every mangy stray on the streets even when it was raining.

Her parents had never bought her a kitten; her school friends were dog people; her work as a photographic model consisted of cat-less sessions under arc lamps or on exotic locations. Occasionally she was asked to pose with a greyhound (she was that kind of model) but never with a cuddly cat.

Though cats played no definite role in her life, she was neverthe-less aware of them. She never passed a cat without a word of greeting; she always bought a cat calendar; the enchanting ways of a tiny kitten in a pet shop window practically melted her heart into her high fashion boots.

At this particular time in her life Lucinda was on an emotional see-saw, being courted, to use an old-fashioned word, by a man who wanted to marry her. She found the situation intolerable because she did not want to get married, even though she loved him as she did. Her freedom and independence were precious. She did not think she could live without them. It was hard to sleep at night with these thoughts chasing her dreams, all of which tended to create fragile blue shadows where blue shadows should not lurk.

'Darling, you're looking tired,' said Marc Lauritzen, the Danish photographer who used her regularly for glossy fashion photos. 'Have I been pushing the work too hard? You know how I get carried away.'

'These coats are hot and heavy,' she said, slipping a hand under the big collar of the long fur to ease it away from her damp neck. The spot lights and reflectors gave off a glaring heat. It was the middle of

49

summer and she was modelling furs. It was a crazy world.

'Would you like to take a quick shower? I can be setting up the next shots. More fake whelk stalls,' he grinned.

The luxury furs were being photographed against barrow boy settings. It was supposed to be amusing. Lucinda thought it was tactless but then she only did what she was told and Marc only photographed as commissioned. He was very professional.

'Lovely,' she said, planting a small moist kiss behind his right ear. 'I'd love a shower.'

'Come back to me gorgeous and smelling of heaven,' he said extravagantly, all Danish charm and gallant confusion.

Marc's flat was on the floor over his photographic studio and dark room. Living above the shop, he called it. Lucinda went up the spiral staircase to his bathroom. She knew her way around his flat since he was the man she loved. He was sensitive, kind, funny and talented. He loved photographing beautiful things and beautiful women like Lucinda. She had strange and haunting eyes . . . large and luminous like green water, flecked with specks of gold. Her cheek bones were narrow and high as if an ancestor had been a Tibetan princess; her long silvery hair spun a halo of magic round her small face.

She was always graceful, with dignity and a sweet nature. It was not surprising that she was a highly paid and successful model.

Lucinda threw off the heavy fur coat, slipped out of her bikini pants and bra and stepped under the shower. Turning the dial to tepid, she tipped her head sideways so that her hair and make-up would not get wet.

As the water touched her skin, it was like an electric shock. She leaped back, cringing against the wall of the shower unit, her nerve cells tingling. The spray fell harmlessly from the nozzle onto her bare feet, but she cried out, moving this way and that to evade the water, curling her toes as spasms shot through her body, whimpering with terror.

Lucinda crouched away from the water, trembling, watching the curtain of hissing steam that, cutting off her escape route, sharpened her fear. It was a crawling feeling that touched all the nerve ends of her skin. At the same time she felt she was almost choked with a terrible premonition of drowning. She was so frightened that for a moment she almost fainted. But she had to get away. She had to steel herself to make a dash through the water. It never occurred to her to turn it off.

As she floundered through the stinging droplets, eyes tightly closed, gasping helplessly, she no longer thought of her hair or her make-up. She stood on the bathmat, shaking, her knees barely holding her up. She did not understand what had happened, but the sensation of horror had been real enough as the water swept over her skin.

It took several minutes to regain her composure. She grabbed at a big towel and began to dry herself, not merely patting the moisture but scrubbing her skin dry. She calmed down and decided that there must be fleas in the fur coat. That must be the explanation. There could be no other. Some microscopic insects must have been nestling in the fur, close to the warmth of her body. Well, she was not wearing that coat again. She slipped into Marc's bathrobe and went downstairs to the studio.

'Have you got enough shots of this coat?' she asked in a voice as near normal as she could manage. She slung the ocelot fur over the clothes rail, and it crouched like a leopard preparing to leap, one sleeve swinging like a feline tail.

'Plenty, darling. Are you all right? You look a little pale. Do you want to stop?'

Lucinda shook her head and found a smile. 'No, I'm fine. I'll just repair my face and hair.'

'I'd like to do the slinky evening dress and the Arctic fox fur cape. Just the right outfit for an evening at a whelk stall,' he grinned.

Lucinda posed for every angle, stretching her limbs, shaking the vinegar, popping a whelk between her glossy lips. They were funny little morsels of coloured fish; she had never eaten one in her life. The first slipped down her throat without her even knowing it. Marc moved round her . . . click, click, click . . . the shutter of his camera sounding like castanets.

'Lucinda! You've eaten the lot. You've eaten all my props! I didn't know you were a whelk gourmet. Perhaps I shan't have to buy you supper now.'

'I'm terribly sorry,' said Lucinda, perplexed. 'I just didn't notice myself eating them. Have I ruined the shots?'

51

Marc began dismantling his equipment. 'Of course not, darling. You are obviously starving yourself again, hence this charming air of abstraction. When are you going to let me look after you permanently and properly?'

'Oh Marc, please . . .' Lucinda was dressing rapidly in the little room allotted to his models. 'I don't want to talk about it, especially today.' The experience in the shower had left her nervous and disorientated. She began filing her nails with an emery board. They were long, filbert-shaped nails and she was proud of them.

'That's what you keep saying, Lucinda, and it's driving me mad. I must know some time.'

She came out of the dressing room in her street clothes, a vision in a hand-dyed cotton prairie skirt with glimpses of lace petticoat, her tiny waist emphasised by a laced-up antique bodice, a twisted scarf of rainbow colours threaded through her silvery hair.

Marc wrapped his arms round her, rocking her close, breathing in the elusive perfume of her skin and hair.

'Don't keep me waiting too long,' he groaned.

He took her to a well-known riverside restaurant that specialised in seafood. Lucinda shivered as she caught sight of the Thames flowing darkly past the terrace. She turned away from the river. She wanted to be somewhere dry and warm.

'Can we eat inside?' she asked, tucking her arm through his. 'I'm feeling a little cold.'

She ordered prawn cocktail and left the lettuce; sole bonne femme and did not touch the accompanying vegetables; strawberries and cream and ignored the fruit. Marc said nothing. It must be some new diet. Models were always dieting.

'Do you think I could have some more cream,' Lucinda said as the sweet trolley went by. The waiter, captivated by her smile, poured cream generously over the strawberries. 'Lovely,' she murmured contentedly.

She felt better after the meal and was able to dismiss the earlier experience from her mind. She curled up to sleep in her bed with Marc's kisses still warm on her lips.

But in the morning, when she turned on her shower, the same electrifying fear shot through her. She watched the water with horror although it was not touching her skin. It splashed harmlessly

52

before running away down the hole. Nothing would make her go into the water. She wrapped a towel round her arm before darting her hand to the controls and turning off the water from source. She leaned against the edge of the washbasin, her head hanging, taking in deep breaths. She could not understand this fear. There were no fleas to blame it on this time. Perhaps it was an allergy. Seafood was always tricky and she had eaten rather a lot. She suddenly remembered the whelks . . . yes, it must be the whelks.

A damp flannel temporarily freshened-up her face and body. She discovered that if she used the cloth with slow, sweeping strokes it was not so alarming. She brushed and brushed her hair, not wanting to risk a shampoo.

That evening Marc took her to a first night at Drury Lane theatre. All the stars were there, but it was Lucinda who was turning heads. She looked ravishing in a 1930s slipper satin gown with trailing ostrich feathers, a diamanté band taking her hair back from her brow, long sparkling ear-rings hanging from her tiny ears.

She did not touch the vodka and ice that he bought her in the bar. There was something about its taste she disliked.

'Darling, I've rented a villa in Cannes for a month. Will you come with me? It would be a wonderful place for a honeymoon. Please think about it . . . you've been working so hard.'

Lucinda thought about it all through the first half of the musical. She sat in the dark, absent-mindedly filing her long nails. She did not want to make this kind of decision, even though she knew she loved Marc. But she needed her freedom and the space to breath. The idea of being tied, even to someone she loved so dearly, made her heart sink. It would be like a prison, taking away the independent spirit which she had always felt so strongly.

The lights went up for the interval and Lucinda blinked open her eyes. Had she fallen asleep? Marc took her hand.

'What a marvellous show. Would you like another drink? I left an order at the bar for your favourite vodka.'

'Could I possibly have an ice cream instead?' she asked.

'It could be wonderful in Cannes,' said Marc, as he kissed her goodnight. 'Swimming all day . . .' Lucinda shuddered involuntarily. That decided Lucinda; definitely no Cannes. 'And fishing for our supper, grilling our own freshly caught fish . . .' Now that

53

sounded more interesting . . .

She could not sleep. She stood in the kitchen of her flat at 2 am, wide awake, her finger in a pot of crab paste. She licked her finger in a worried and abstract way. This aversion to water was beginning to make life difficult. Baths were totally out. She had leaped into a shower like a demented kangaroo, hating even that brief contact with water. She was using gallons of cleansing cream, and she had bought paper plates and cups to save doing any washing up. How strange her life was becoming and she could not understand it. Perhaps she ought to see a doctor. It could be her hormones.

After drinking a glass of milk, she nibbled at some raw liver she had bought to make pâté; then she went back to her bedroom. Only she did not go to bed. Instead she curled up at the foot of the bed and went to sleep under the duvet.

The doctor referred her to a specialist. He thought it was a psychological reaction to her work where the emphasis was on beauty and cleanliness.

'You are fighting against your own image,' he said, pleased with the neat phrase. He wrote it down for future use.

The clever words did not help Lucinda to adjust to this dread of water. One day she sat crouched on her fire escape in the rain, just tolerating the fine mist. Her face was hidden against her knees, rain dripping down her hair. A small soft padded paw touched her ankle tentatively. It was a little ginger creature, drops of rain on its whiskers like pearls, its bright eyes questioning and curious.

'Hello,' whispered Lucinda, her fingers stroking the wet fur gently. 'Isn't it a strange world, cat?'

The cat looked at her with unblinking concern. There was nothing it could do to help her.

'Wake up darling. You've dropped off again,' said Marc as he caught her napping for the third time in a morning. Lucinda yawned and stretched her spine deliciously.

'I've discovered I have the knack of dropping off to sleep for a moment and then waking up quite refreshed,' she said lightly. 'It seems perfectly natural.' She got to her feet from the studio floor and began to prowl round the set, then came over to Marc and nuzzled her face against her arm. 'Have you got any milk?' she asked.

'Shall I make some coffee?' he offered.

She shook her head, scratching her ear. 'I've gone right off coffee. Just milk . . . unless you've got some cream?'

'Gold top,' he promised.

She slept less and less at night and took to walking. She found she could see perfectly well in the dark with no need to take a torch, and she was never afraid. And her fear of heights seemed to have left her. One night she walked along the parapet of London Bridge without a qualm, with only the ghostly Tower Bridge and the steely HMS Belfast to witness her feat of balance.

She huddled against the stone lions guarding the base of Cleopatra's Needle on the Embankment. There were all kinds of legends about the tall obelisk, stories of hauntings and ghosts that returned to the place where they had leaped into the Thames. She wondered if the cold stone missed the warmth of sunny Heliopolis where it had once stood 3,500 years ago . . . her clothes felt hot and itchy and she longed to take them off, removing the leather belt of her coat and letting it slip to the ground. How tightly her shoes pinched her toes; they were heavy and she eased them off.

Marc had the opportunity to buy a week-end cottage with a marvellous view of the Mendip Hills. He could get it for a bargain price and his bank would give him a generous mortgage.

'But I'm not going ahead until I know definitely that we are going to be together,' he pressed.

'Of course we'll be together,' she said lovingly.

'I mean married,' he said, his mouth taking on a firm line. 'It's time we came to some decision, Lucinda.'

'Oh no, please,' said Lucinda. 'Please don't make me decide between you.'

'Between you? What do you mean? Is there someone else?'

'No . . .' Lucinda said unhappily. 'I meant you and my freedom, my independence.'

'You meant another man.' Marc was hurt and angry. 'Now I understand why you have been so difficult to pin down. I should have known. Perhaps there are dozens of men in your life.'

Lucinda was shocked at his unfair accusation and the grim, uncaring look in his eyes. She rushed at him with her nails drawn. He caught her wrists in mid-air, astounded at her sudden turn on him, and held her away in an iron grip.

'You little hell cat,' he rasped. 'Don't you dare use your nails on me!'

Lucinda wrenched herself out of his grip and ran from him. Marc had never lost his temper before, nor ever spoken to her so roughly. She did not know where to go to hide the hurt. Tears choked her as she fled into the dark streets, not caring where she went. The wind lifted her hair and she felt as if she was falling into a bowl of stars . . .

It was all becoming too much, these strange fears of water and her changing habits. How could she cope with this illness, and at the same time make decisions which would affect the rest of her life? She fought the tightness of panic . . .

Her vision blurred, her thoughts, confused and incoherent, seemed unable to recognise anything as familiar. The streets were longer and the buildings grew taller in the night air. She lost her way, blundering through alleys she did not know. Blindly she ran along the Embankment, stumbling over the uneven flag stones, scattering a beer can. It rolled away into the gutter with a loud clatter. Somewhere she dropped her handbag and the pretty things spilled onto the pavement. Somewhere near the tall looming obelisk, she just . . . disappeared.

It was in all the newspapers.

FAMOUS MODEL VANISHES

They printed photographs of her modelling the long ocelot coat with the lynx collar. They wrote snappy stories about her rise to fame and the pressure of a model's life style. The police found her handbag and some of its contents scattered near Cleopatra's Needle, and frogmen began searching the muddy water of the Thames. Some small boys found her leather belt when the tide went out.

Everyone came to the same sad conclusion. Cleopatra's Needle, shrouded in night mist, had a long history of suicides and mysterious, unexplained happenings.

Marc was stunned. He held a sombre farewell exhibition of Lucinda's photographs because there could not be any kind of funeral. Her lovely face gazed at him from the walls, the golden-flecked eyes and silvery hair more ephemeral than ever.

Marc went back to his work and tried to numb his mind with punishing schedules. His new model, Vicky, was hopeless. He could not get the right angles of light for her face. After several unproductive sessions, they agreed that Marc should phone the agency to send someone else.

He held open the door for Vicky to leave and in walked a thin silvery white cat, blinking brilliant green eyes. It walked straight in as if it owned the place, climbed onto the dais and began grooming its fluffy fur.

'Good heavens, what a gorgeous cat,' said Vicky. 'Is it yours?'

'No, I've never seen it before. It must be a stray, but it seems to know its way around.'

'It looks to me as if you are being adopted,' said Vicky, straightening the seams of her stockings. 'Don't you know about cats? They always choose their owners, not the other way round.'

Marc grinned briefly. 'Really? I didn't know that. Good-bye then, Vicky, and thanks for coming. I'm sorry it didn't work out.'

As he cleared away his equipment, he became aware of the cat staring at him with solemn eyes, watching his every movement.

'I'm going through a rough time,' he said conversationally. 'I can't seem to work without my darling Lucinda.'

The cat jumped down from the dais and wound itself sympathetically round Marc's ankles, its back arched gracefully, little paws so dainty and light, kneading the air.

'You're a pretty little thing,' said Marc, going down on a knee to touch the soft fur. 'Would you like some milk?'

A tiny throaty purr began to vibrate, and the sound was joyous and unexpected.

'Gold top?' he promised.

The cat stretched up, one paw on his knee, and nuzzled his face with a small, moist nose. It tickled and Marc had to laugh. The light from the studio arc lamps turned the cat's fur into a silvery halo, sparks of light shooting into space.

The artistic possibilities suddenly took Marc's breath away. This gentle, intelligent cat was the most beautiful creature.

'I think I'll call you Cindy,' he said, gently lifting the furry chin with one finger. 'Will you be my new model? I need you.'

The gold-flecked eyes deepened and gazed at him with unconcealed love. She had no more decisions to make.

The Bad Luck Cat

Judy Gardiner

The Pastecka family had lived in the shadow of the mountain for three generations and it seemed to the eldest daughter that their luck would never change until they moved to a better place. Here, the iron cold of the winter lasted for nine months of the year, and the brief summers, flaring a sudden dry heat, tended to scorch even the oats and the rye. As for the hens, they would crouch panting inside the doorway of the one-room dwelling, too deep in lethargy even to lay an egg.

And the family had become equally inert. No one bothered to work hard any more except the eldest daughter, and although she constantly upbraided them for Godless indolence she knew that the real cause of their relentless poverty was due to living on the wrong side of the mountain. On the other side the winters would be mild, the summers temperate, and the goats would yield rich milk. Sometimes, chopping wood or carrying pails of water from the river, she would allow herself the luxury of a daydream about living in a house that had a watertap just outside the door.

On the other side of the mountain there was said to be a railway line leading to a big city where women wore silk stockings and drank wine in cafés, but the eldest daughter had no means of verifying such rumours. In any case, wine-sipping and silk stockings were of little interest to her compared with a decent crop of cabbages or enough goat's milk to make a couple of extra cheeses to lay in for the winter. No one worked, let alone practised constructive thinking, except her.

The Pastecka family had six members. A toothless grandmother, an uncle simple from birth, the father and his three daughters. The father, a taciturn man with big fists and a small skull, had been a widower for ten years and his two younger girls disliked him because he made no attempt to find them husbands; on the subject of husbands, the eldest daughter maintained a thin-lipped silence.

Living in close proximity to them all were eight hens, a milking goat and a one-eared black and white cat. The cat had arrived uninvited from God knows where, sidling in at the door one bitter March night and creeping on its belly towards the fire. The eldest daughter wanted to shoo it out, but the uncle who was simple dropped some rabbit bones on the floor for it, and giggled when it seized them and shot away with them into a dark corner. The cat stayed, and the family became accustomed to its presence while remaining indifferent to its welfare. As for the animal itself, it managed its own affairs with quiet competence, stealing a little food here and a little warmth there, and allaying human anger by catching rats in the grain store.

The cat had been living as part of the Pastecka family for six months when the landlord decided to double the already exorbitant rent he was charging for the mean hovel and one hectare of stony ground. The father swore but did nothing, the old grandmother beseeched the Virgin for help and the two younger daughters cried in one another's arms. Looking at them all, and at the uncle who simpered uncomprehendingly, the eldest daughter flung on her headscarf and marched round to the landlord's house.

He told her that he needed the money for his daughter's dowry.

'You're lying. No man in his right senses would take your daughter for a whole barrel of money.'

'Jealous are you, my poor creature?'

'The day I become jealous of her pudding face and rotten teeth is the day I drown myself in the river.'

'Get out,' the landlord said, raising his fist. 'Get out before I have you evicted for insolence.'

The eldest daughter looked at him with contempt. Don't worry about evicting us,' she said, 'because we're going anyway.'

'Going?' He dropped his fist. 'Where to, if one may ask?'

'To a new place. An influential friend of long standing has invited us to live rent-free in one of his properties. The climate is mild, the soil is productive and there is even water from a tap outside the door.'

'And where is this marvellous place to be found, except in heaven?' He was laughing unrestrainedly.

'On the other side of the mountain,' said the eldest daughter. 'I just called to advise you that we are packed and ready to start.'

'So we go in three days' time,' she told the family at supper. 'I have arranged it.'

'Going? Leaving here? But why? They stared at her blankly, soup spoons raised halfway to mouths.

'Because I think it's best.'

'Perhaps you've no objection to telling us where we're supposed to be going?' The father strove for sarcasm.

'The other side of the mountain. Over there the land is better and there are more hours of daylight to work in.'

'I heard of a man who went over the mountain,' he said uneasily. 'And he never came back.'

'Only a fool would come back to a place like this.'

For a moment she was tempted to tell them of the dream she had had for so long; the dream of plenty born out of a lifetime's penury, but she said nothing. Neither did she tell them that it was a row with the landlord that had precipitated the dream into sudden reality.

One of her sisters ventured to ask how they would make the journey.

'By walking, unless you have an alternative to suggest.'

Hands clasped, the old grandmother began to pray in a sibilant whisper while the uncle broke off a piece of rye bread and aimed it at the cat. The eldest daughter slapped his arm.

'If you must throw things at the creature throw a stone, not food.'

He put his thumb in his mouth and giggled.

The other daughter asked if they would be taking the hens.

'Of course. We'll put them in a crate and load them in the handcart. The goat will have to walk like the rest of us.'

'What about the cat?'

'The cat stays behind,' the eldest daughter said. 'And must fend for itself.'

And within a very short while the cat began to realise that something strange was about to happen. Not only the bustle of packing, the stripping of the poor little dwelling down to its flimsy walls and hard earth floor, but something in the very atmosphere itself troubled and alarmed it. It sat alone in the thin September sunlight as the handcart was loaded with bedding and cooking pots and then finally with the fluttering hens in their rough wooden crate.

They left without bothering to close the door, a little tight-knit group in rough dark clothes, and they didn't look back. The cat watched them grow smaller and smaller and listened as the plaintive cry of the goat grew fainter until it died into silence. Inside the house the ashes from the fire were still warm and there was still a lingering smell of cabbage soup, but everything else had gone.

The cat moistened the side of its paw with saliva then passed it over the place where its ear had been. It washed its cheeks, scrubbed for a moment or two at the white whiskers of its eyebrows, then settled down to wait for the Pasteckas' return.

On the third day after their departure the silence was broken by the landlord's arrival. He came by horse and cart, and when the cat heard the harsh grating of wheels it fled out into the fields. The landlord spent some time looking round the place; kicking at lumps of earth and prodding the dirty straw that still remained in the goat's lean-to shack as if expecting to uncover his vanished tenants. Peering through the ripening thistle heads the cat watched him come out of the dwelling and fasten the door with a padlock before climbing back into the cart and chuck-chucking to the horse to proceed on its way.

The wind was sharpening and the nights were carrying the first hint of frost when the cat decided to follow the Pasteckas.

It stood close to the spot where they had all assembled that morning, staring in the direction they had taken and raising its nostrils for a scent of them. Then it began to walk, slinking close to the hedgerow where the winter berries were ripening and the swifts were twittering about the coming journey south. The mountain range stretched ahead, soaking the landscape in blue shadow, and every now and then the cat would pause with one foot uplifted while it tested the air with expanded nostrils. There was no scent of the family, yet it trusted the instinct that declared this route to be the correct one.

On the following day it caught a young rabbit. Too hungry to torment it, the cat killed with a swift bite at the jugular, then dragged the carcass to the privacy of some bushes. It ate without haste, disposing of the creature in its entirety before washing its face and forepaws and then coiling neat as a snail in the forked branches of a rowan tree.

It walked in moonlight, the cold wind blowing down from the mountains, flattening its fur against its body. But the wind also brought a faint hint of the Pasteckas on its breath, and the cat raised its head and widened its nostrils receptively. The country became rougher, and before long the scent of the Pasteckas was obliterated by other more disquieting ones. Aware that it was moving through hostile territory the cat sought to unravel and then to identify the rank, invisible trails that crossed its path; fox certainly, and badger mingled with the shrill odour of weasel and stoat. But there were others too; heavy pungent scents that spoke to the cat of large animals hungry for warm blood and melting flesh.

The old savage days of kill or be killed, eat or be eaten, came back to it and it hurried on its way, intent only on outpacing the shadows and their fearful hints. Then with the dwindling of trees and scrub the air grew thinner and the cold increased. The cat's mind became blank and it no longer remembered why it was travelling. Like some small and obdurate machine it continued to pick its way between the sharp boulders, sleeping little and eating less. The first flakes of snow fell and a buzzard preparing for migration soared in slow thoughtful circles above the cat's path. The cat slipped itself into a small crevasse and waited until the bird had passed.

It took many many days to cross the mountain and many more to locate the Pastecka family. The first memories began to return at the scent of woodsmoke drifting from a gipsy's fire and at the sight of washing impaled on a hedge to dry. With blistered feet and claws worn down, the cat limped into the muddy little yard where the eight hens were clustered round the Pasteckas' doorway. Suddenly unsure of its welcome it hid itself behind an old handcart, waiting for darkness.

Then it slipped gaunt as a shadow into the house, and one of the two younger daughters caught sight of it and cried out in wonderment that the cat should have followed them all the way over the mountain.

'It can't be the same one –'

'It is – it is! It's only got one ear – '

The girl fed the cat with a bowl of rye bread soaked in mutton gravy and the uncle stuck his finger in his mouth and giggled.

They seemed to find something remarkable, even a little touching, in the cat's evident determination to remain part of the family. Only the eldest daughter sat with her rough tired hands in her lap and regarded the animal with misgiving.

Because already her bright dreams of a better life on the other side of the mountain were paling into disillusion. Although it was warmer, the rain fell day after day and the old grandmother caught a fever, and the family's pleasure in settling in a place where there were neighbours was shortlived. For it hadn't occurred to the eldest daughter that on the other side of the mountain it was another country, where they spoke a different language and seemed disinclined to accept strangers. Although they made signs that the Pastecka family could avail itself of the empty hovel on the edge of the village they made no attempt to show them the way of things. On the contrary, someone threw stones at the uncle because he was simple and they laughed at the eldest daughter because she wore men's boots.

Only one man spoke to them, stumblingly, in their own language, and like the eldest daughter he too seemed obsessed by the dream of a better life elsewhere. With a small pinched face sheltered by a baggy cap he would pass the time of day with her sometimes when she was trudging back from the well with the two water buckets, suspended from their wooden yoke, dragging at her shoulders.

'There must be a better life away from this place. Here the soil's exhausted, everything rots with the damp and the government does not keep faith with the people. They promised us a railway, but the nearest one is still a walk of fifteen miles from here.'

'I don't care about railways,' said the eldest daughter. 'My first priority is to have a water tap outside the door.'

'Railways are vital,' the man said, trudging along beside her. 'They mean freedom. They mean transportation to cities, where there is work of a gentler kind. In cities there is a choice of occupation. There is electricity, water comes from nowhere except out of taps, and the women – ' he glanced down at her bare red legs and men's boots 'the woman are said to wear silk stockings.'

'I have no need of silk stockings,' the eldest daughter said repressively, but the old dream, the old longing for a better way of life began to torment her again. It pricked at her nerves and drew her lips into a thin hard line.

She thought about the man's words that night, lying on the straw palliasse she shared with the old grandmother, who was shivering and muttering in delirium. From the other side of the room the father shouted to her to shut up . . .

In a city there would be a hospital where the poor old girl would either get better or die in comfort. There would be work other than toiling in the fields and there would be a chance for the two younger girls to find husbands. Nice husbands, thought the eldest daughter, who would not be brutalised by the hard ways of subsistence farming. As for her, she wanted no man, and no love other than the reasonable respect of a family that had been guided by her into a world of improved living standards.

A few weeks later the man who spoke their language met her again, and said in a low excited voice: 'I spoke ill of our government too soon. They are keeping faith with us after all, and have devised a scheme whereby we may apply for work in the cities. They will provide houses and jobs and education for our children –'

'How do we get there?'

'By railway train,' the man said gleefully. 'We walk the fifteen miles and then we can take the railway train. It is all arranged.'

'How many are going?'

'All those who have intelligence.'

'It makes sense. But we will probably be excluded because we are foreigners.'

The man's brightness faded a little. 'True. But if you were to say –'

'And besides, we have no papers.'

'Perhaps they will provide them.'

'Who knows?' said the eldest daughter with a wry smile. 'Although I doubt it. It wouldn't be our luck.'

But in the meantime the cat was happy. Stealthily reinstated, it spent a lot of time lying curled in the shadow of the grandmother's long woollen skirt while the tiredness passed slowly from its limbs and the blisters healed on its feet. Fellow convalescents, the animal and the old woman seemed to draw a wordless encouragement from one another, and the younger daughter who attended to the cooking would surreptitiously spoon a little bread and soup into a cracked saucer and put it down on the floor by her grandmother's feet.

So far as the cat was concerned there was very little difference between the old home and the new. The first had been made of clapboard through which the wind had howled and the snowflakes whirled, and the second was made of stone through which the eternal damp seeped and spread the walls with a delicate green fungus. But a fire still slumbered on the hearth, the smell of slow peasant cooking was the same, and the voices that rose and fell were those of the Pastecka family. So far as the cat was concerned, either place was beyond criticism.

The winter was well advanced before it became aware of a subtle change in the atmosphere. Drowsily it listened to the voice of the eldest daughter, the low monotone rising every now and then to a sharp scolding when anyone interrupted. From the shelter of the grandmother's skirt the cat watched the father bring his big adamant fist down on the table with a crash that made the uncle giggle and the two younger girls start apprehensively. The eldest daughter began to pace up and down with her arms folded tightly against her chest. The voices rose, shutting out the sound of sobbing wind and drumming rain.

When the grandmother got up from her chair and hobbled towards her half of the straw palliasse the fire flames had died, the ashes had cooled, and the only thing that seemed to remain was the voice of the eldest daughter, persuading, exhorting, bullying. No one was arguing with her any more, and from its place in the corner the cat was oppressed by a sick sense of foreboding.

The packing was done, the hens re-crated, the handcart loaded. Tethered close to the door in readiness, the goat bleated as if its dim wits were groping to comprehend a situation of terrible complexity.

But the cat understood. Deep in its entrails it had recognised the pattern; the stripping of the house, the voices warm with optimism and the vivacious twirling of the two younger girls as if in expectation of something particularly wonderful. From its humble place on the floor it read in the Pastecka faces the hope of a new future. And this time, it was prepared.

It watched the cracked saucer which it had so often polished loving-clean with its tongue, being slipped into a box that held clothes and bits of bedding.

'We won't need that.'

'It's the cat's – '

'The cat isn't coming – '

'Oh – *why?* . . .' The young girl's vivacity fading.

'They don't have cats in cities, you fool. And besides . . .'

And besides, thought the eldest daughter, the cat brings bad luck. Nothing has gone right for us since it first arrived. I hate all cats, and particularly that one.

'Suppose it follows us?'

'What, on a train?'

The girl showed signs of arguing but the eldest sister clenched her bony fists and said 'For God's sake stop worrying about trivialities. It's hard enough being responsible for a family of human beings without fussing over a useless animal.'

'The cat isn't useless!'

'Does it give milk or lay eggs?'

The girl had to admit that it didn't.

A sudden knocking on the door made them start. It was the man who had first introduced them to the government scheme for moving people to the cities, and he spoke to the eldest daughter in a rapid whisper.

'Don't worry about not having the right papers. A lot of us are going from here and there'll be a lot more waiting at the railway. You'll be able to mingle with the crowd and there'll be no trouble . . .'

No trouble, thought the eldest daughter when the man had gone. All we ever have is trouble. Aloud, she said: 'Where's the cat? I won't have it following us this time.'

But the cat had vanished.

They left soon after, the old grandmother leaning heavily on her stick and her father cursing the goat for pulling on its chain. They joined the other villagers who had decided to leave for the city and yet they remained apart, trudging along with eyes cast down because they had no papers and didn't speak the language. At the head of the procession there was laughter and even some snatches of song, the sound blowing eerily in the wind. A thin hard snow, spiteful as flung gravel, began coating the bowed figures and the Pastecka father put his chapped lips close to his eldest girl's headscarf and said: 'Well, let's hope you're right this time. You certainly weren't the time before.'

'If we depended on you,' she said, 'we'd have starved long ago.'

They reached the railway as dusk was falling, and many of them exclaimed in wonderment at the huge engine hissing and gasping and blowing bursts of white steam at the head of its coaches.

As the man had said, the Pastecka family had no trouble because of the lack of papers; the only trouble was in trying to keep together among the crowd that pushed and shoved and laughed and swore over the business of loading in their live beasts and bedding, howling babies and babbling old folk. The government had had to remove the seats from the carriages in order to accommodate the happy torrent of household goods and the Pasteckas were grateful for the straw-strewn floor where their closely-guarded goat lay cosily against someone else's pig.

A great cheer went up as the train gave its first convulsive lurch forward, and the eldest Pastecka daughter clenched her hard cold hands together and thought: The city – the city! Bright lights and running water. A warm house for us and a dry cellar for the animals . . .

The night passed contentedly, everyone swaying in unison to the fascinating diddle-de-dum rhythm of the train. The Pastecka family slept sitting on the floor back to back, chins resting on knees, and an hour before dawn the cat crept out of the haystack in which it had hidden itself. Stretching its cramped limbs, it located the harsh scent of home-made sausage and helped itself, neatly extracting the slices from between the rough cut hunks of bread while the owner slept. Satisfied, it crept back to its place of hiding.

The eldest daughter awoke, rubbing her stiff neck and grimacing at the foetid air. In a sensible attempt to conserve heat the government had fitted the train windows with wooden shutters, which left whatever light there might be to filter through the chinks. She sat quietly, contemplating the darkly shrouded forms huddled around her and thinking that every jolt, every rattling, clattering diddle-de-dum was carrying them nearer the city.

Then in the gloom she saw the haysack move. Instantly suspecting that a rat had found its way into the goat's fodder she watched through narrowed eyes, and when a brief flicker of moonlight illuminated the black and white face of the cat nosing cautiously out, incredulity turned to furious rage.

She grabbed at it, missed – grabbed again, and the cat gave a squawk that made the old grandmother moan in her sleep. Lurching stiffly from her place, the eldest daughter tightened her grip on the scruff of the cat's neck and stumbled towards the window. People were packed so closely together that it was difficult to avoid stepping on them.

With her free hand she began wrenching at the shutter, trying to unfasten it. It resisted. Panting, she drove her fist where a chink of pale light filtered through. She swore, spitting out the words as her mind crowded with images of bad luck. The cold, the hunger, the incessant toil that brought no reward. And the cat, malevolence personified, was at the root of it all. Nothing had gone right since it had first crept over the threshold.

Her pounding fist splintered the wood and she broke a small section away with bloodstained fingers. As if anticipating her intention the cat screamed, and tried to hurl its dangling body upwards towards her arm. She lifted it in both hands, holding it by the throat as if she proposed to strangle it, and for a long desperate moment she and the cat stared into the dark glitter of one another's eyes. Then with a quick movement she thrust the animal through the hole in the shutter, cramming it, shoving it, and tugging its frantic claws from her sleeve. And then she felt emptiness, a sudden void, as the cat disappeared.

She remained at the aperture in the shutter for some time, drinking in the stinging east wind and letting it blow cold on her face, on her rage and on her fear. The train's rhythm began slowing to a gentle diddle-de-diddle-de-diddle, and with one cold-blurred eye she was able to see the first dazzling white lights of the city.

Her heart stopped its agitated pounding and she returned to her place on the floor, stepping over the goat and stumbling over her father's outstretched legs. All around them people were waking, and further down the train a cockerel began to crow with sudden marvellous optimism.

'How much longer?' The father rasped his hand over his stubbled cheeks.

'We're almost there,' she said gaily, 'I've already seen the bright lights!'

The moon died and the daylight strengthened. Grey gave way to ice blue, yet the lights of the city maintained their hard white stare. They illuminated the low huts and the high watchtowers, the soaring chimney and the barbed wire.

A mile away, the cat shook off the last clouds of concussion. It stood staring in the direction of the train, of the city, with raised head and probing nostrils, then sickened by the charnel house stench it turned and began the long lonely journey back home.

Tico

Mark Ronson

'*I just don't believe it,*' *the commander of the NASA spacecraft* Pioneer
II *muttered as he stepped onto the surface of the new planet with the
metallic replica of Old Glory ready for the claiming ceremony.*

Pioneer II *had touched down on a smooth, sandy plain which ran to a
horizon made jagged by majestic snow peaks. But it was not the landscape
which astonished the small party of earthpersons – it was that they found
themselves in an avenue of titanic stones, each of which had been carved
into an image that was ridiculously familiar.*

'*They can't be,*' *began the pretty communications officer.*

'*Oh yes, they are,*' *the expedition biologist said.* '*They're pussy cats all
right!*'

The shuttle docked perfectly with the starclipper hanging peacefully
in the orbit in which she had been assembled. The incoming crew
made their way through the airlock, each carrying the single grip of
personal belongings NASA allowed. These held family video discs,
micro-books and some oddly touching mementos such as a lock of
hair, a pressed flower or, in one case, a small bag of sand from Bondi
Beach – sentimental bric-a-brac to reminisce over during the voyage
to the rim of the solar system.

As the circular door hissed shut behind them the faces of several
twitched. How much terrestrial time would elapse before it slid open
again?

In the clinical reception area, lined with emergency space suits like
rows of mummified divers, a loudspeaker ordered the ship's company to assemble in the mess.

'Now for it,' said Dr Pamela Byrd, the ship's psychosurgeon.
'Face to face with the enigma at last.'

The others grinned uneasily. During their training period at Space Centre rumours of their captain's eccentricity had been rife. Some claimed that he actually prayed in a crisis, others that his view of discipline would have delighted Captain Bligh while darker stories hinted at physical peculiarities. The most outrageous of the latter was that he was part android following the burn-out on the ill-fated Martian landing of which he had been the sole survivor.

Although the crew had never set foot in the clipper, they knew it intimately through their instruction in the Space Centre replica. Without a second thought they trooped down a corridor – well padded in case the artificial gravity system should malfunction – and into the messroom. The central table was set out with glasses and champagne bottles rimed from the refrigerator. At the head of it stood a stocky, silver-bearded man in a reefer jacket with brass buttons such as Victorian sea captains wore.

What made his crew gaze in silent wonder was not his seamed face – colourless since that radiation blast on Mars – but the small black cat perched on his shoulder, a cat which on Earth would be known as a Foreign Black.

Snow Ryan, the Australian hydroponics expert, caught Pamela Byrd's eye and whispered, 'It's flamin' well true, the skipper's a refugee from Mad Island. Bet he thinks that cat's a flamin' parrot!'

With a bloodless grimace which passed for a smile, the man at the table regarded the dozen members of his crew for a long minute and then announced, 'I am Captain John Hellyer, and I am happy to welcome you aboard *Pioneer*. I regret that we have not met before but it was essential that I was here during construction. However, I do know you from your dossiers and I am sure we shall become better acquainted in the watches which lie ahead.' Suddenly he turned to Pamela. 'Did you get your golf simulator loaded, doctor?'

'Yes, thank you, captain. I want to have a shot at the Ladies' Open when I get back.'

'When my grandfather was a sea captain – and his father before him – it was the custom to drink toasts in treacle-thick rum,' Hellyer resumed. 'But times change, and as half my crew are of what was once known as the fair sex, I thought Tattinger would be more appropriate. So let's break it out and drink a toast.'

Champagne corks bounced off the ceiling, but the eyes of the crew

71

never left the cat balanced on the captain's shoulder. He was so at ease there he must have used this perch since he was a kitten.

'I want to propose a toast to our starclipper, the most beautiful and sophisticated piece of technology that our species has ever devised,' Hellyer said. 'In the last century man's greatest achievement was the wooden clipper ships with such graceful lines they crossed the oceans like wild birds. The *Lightning* often raced over four hundred nautical miles in a day, while my great-grandfather's ship – coincidentally called *Pioneer* – once made the passage from Shanghai to London in a hundred days.

'Since those great days we have made the quantum leap in technology, and we are privileged to serve on this ultimate expression of that leap. I give you *Pioneer*.'

Glasses clinked and the cat regarded the company with slitted eyes. An embarrassed silence hung in the mess, and sensing it Hellyer said, 'Recharge your glasses and follow me please.'

They did so, glancing at each other and raising their eyebrows.

Hellyer strode up to the bridge under a transparent dome which gave the crew a breath-catching view of the blue and green Earth floating above them.

As their eyes adjusted to the earthlight they gazed about them curiously. The bridge, with its banks of equipment nicknamed the Manhattan Skyline because of its myriad warning lights, was as they remembered it from the Space Centre simulator apart from one object. In place of the conventional navigation console was an old-fashioned ship's wheel made of brass and teak.

'It was my wish to have the manual control in the form of this wheel which came from my great-grandfather's clipper,' Hellyer explained. 'I prefer to touch genuine wood rather than plastic buttons. Doctor, you look as though you have a question?'

'Yes, sir. Uh – is that a real cat on your shoulder?'

He nodded.

'Uh, captain . . . as I understand it, Article 127d of Spaceclipper Regulations – uh – prohibits . . .'

' . . . the carrying of unauthorized animals into space,' Hellyer interrupted. 'You are correct, doctor, although it is, in fact, Article 127g.'

Silence hung in the dome.

'That is what I thought the regulations said,' Pamela said finally.

The captain looked past her with an almost dreamy expression.

'The ship's cat on my great-grandfather's clipper was named Tico,' he said. 'The crew swore that he brought luck.'

'So this chap has the same name,' said Electronics Engineer William Davidson. 'It must have been quite a feat to smuggle him aboard . . .'

As though sensing the captain's surge of anger Tico leapt from his shoulder on to an old fashioned leather pilot's chair.

'Mr Davidson, let it be understood that I would never be a party to the breaking of regulations aboard my own – aboard a NASA space vessel,' Hellyer said in an austere voice. 'If you, sir, were to check the crew register you would find Tico's name entered as a legal crew member with the honorary rank of lieutenant.'

Hellyer's death's head features relaxed as he added, 'He also has the privilege of special rations.'

'But does the register state that Tico is a feline?' someone was bold enough to ask.

'Strangely enough, the bureaucrats who drafted our documentation never thought of questioning the species of crew members so the question never arose.'

There was laughter, some clapping and for the moment the social ice was broken. Several crew members formed an admiring group round Tico. A hand stroked his fur which gleamed like oiled ebony, a finger tickled his ear and he responded with a high-powered purr.

The attention he enjoyed was broken when the voice of the shuttle commander crackled from the sound system. 'Permission to seal the airlock and complete de-docking procedure, captain.'

'Permission to proceed,' Hellyer replied.

'Thank you. And good luck, *Pioneer*.'

A minute later the crew watched the white triangle of the shuttle fall away above their heads.

There was a long silence, then Tico jumped to the floor and scratched his ear vigorously

From a pocket inside his reefer, Hellyer produced a stout packet decorated with red wax.

'Before we set sail it is my duty to break open our sealed orders and inform you of our true destination,' he said. 'I can understand your surprise as NASA announced that the object of our voyage was to visit the outer planets of the Solar System, Neptune and Pluto. That, I fear, was a red herring for the benefit of the East Bloc who have been taking an over-keen interest in our space programme. Our real mission will be outlined in this envelope.'

He opened it and unfolded a sheet of paper while the crew remained uneasy and silent.

'Our destination is our nearest star neighbour Proxima Centuari, the third brightest seen on Earth and a mere 4.29 light years distant,' he told them. 'Our new orbiting telescope discovered it has a planetary system which contains an Earth-type planet now code-named Terra Nova. It will be our task to investigate it with the ultimate aim of colonization.'

He paused and looked at the shocked faces before him. When Pamela spoke she said what was on every mind, 'But we won't live long enough for such a journey.'

Hellyer smiled as his great-grandfather must have done when warned there was ice ahead.

'Have no fear,' he said. 'Tico will only be middle-aged when we make planetfall. *Pioneer* has much more speed than has been admitted. By riding the solar wind we shall travel almost at the speed of light, and should reach our destination in roughly five terrestrial years.

'All of you have been picked for exceptional qualities and you volunteered to undertake exceptional duties. Therefore I am sure that in a short while your thinking will have adapted to this challenge. I shall give you a proper briefing after you have settled into your accommodation. Now I am going to get underway, there is no time to be lost.'

The crew stared at the thousand-metre titanium masts, radiating from *Pioneer's* hull like the spokes of an umbrella, which were visible through the dome. At the touch of Hellyer's fingers on a series of controls the great sails linked to the masts began to rise. The Earthlight caught them and they shone silver.

Made of carbon fibres woven into gossamer fabric, they were designed to catch the vast currents of ionized particles flowing from the sun known as the solar wind. This plasma, which had been discovered by *Mariner 2* in 1962, would propel *Pioneer* across the deeps of space without any energy requirement from the star-clipper.

Even before the sails were taut the watchers saw their home world slide out of sight as the vessel became alive and turned into the plasma stream. Instead of the beautiful planet with its swirls of cloud, they beheld the utter blackness of space arched by a bridge of crushed crystal – the billion motes of unwinking light which made up the Milky Way. The cold immensity of it held them in silence. Only Tico remained unmoved. Tail erect, he strolled down to the galley where he knew the automatic vending machine would have filled his bowl with its regular ration of synthi-milk.

Hellyer's hands fastened on to the spokes of the big ship's wheel.

'Just as the old clippers rode the wind, so we shall drive with the solar wind,' he said. 'Once away from the solar system there will be cross-currents caused by plasma from other stars, maelstroms and trade winds and doldrums . . . perhaps cosmic storms. And it will be Man against the elements as it was on the great clipper routes.'

The captain hauled the wheel over, the sails bellied between the masts and the solar wind tore them out of Earth's orbit.

In space there is no night or day. Time is an abstract measured by the human heartbeat or the dancing figures on the ship's digital chronometers. The *Pioneer's* crew measured their lives by the terrestrial hours spent in various occupations – the watches in which they attended to the running of the ship, the performance of routine experiments, group recreation sessions with the mess transformed into a disco, and private relaxation periods when they read old letters or entered into new love affairs.

But as the digital chronometers became more and more meaningless the crew grew increasingly dispirited. Passion withered under the terrible knowledge that even brief escape from an emotional situation – no matter how agreeable – was impossible. The disco strobes flashed in an empty room, and even the classical music tapes became stale when each note could be anticipated.

The only two unaffected by the creeping ennui were Tico and his captain. The crew's discontent found expression in resentment against the old man who dined alone on the bridge and only left it to check on their unenthusiastic efficiency.

When *Pioneer* was racing on a steady gale of plasma a million light minutes from earth, Snow Ryan lay on the examination couch for his routine health check in Pamela Byrd's surgery.

'Everything seems to be fine physically,' she said. 'It must be your hydroponics which keep us all so fit. Nothing worrying you?'

'Nothing apart from a little confusion as to whether I'm on a spaceship or a flamin' China tea clipper,' he said. 'Whenever I see the Old Man I break out into a sweat in case I haven't holy-stoned the decks properly . . . It was tough enough to suddenly find that I'd be pushing middle-age by the time I saw Oz again, but being under the command of Captain Ahab is the giddy limit. And if I feel like this only halfway out, I reckon I'll be certifiable when we get into Earth orbit again.'

'What makes you think we ever will?' came a sardonic voice and Wilbur Mantell, the expedition archivist, strolled in.

'This is supposed to be a private clinic and I have a patient here,' Pamela said crisply. 'And also I've had enough of your gloom-and-doom talk.'

'What gloom-and-doom talk?' Snow asked.

'Simply this, my old Down Under chum,' said Wilbur. 'Has it occurred to you that while we're outward bound we have the solar wind behind us, but it will be against us on the return voyage? We don't carry near enough fuel to use auxiliary motors, so it is obvious that, whether we like it or not, we are to be the members of the first Terra Nova settlement. We will be used to establish colony rights for the Free World. The sexes divide equally, so there'll be no problem about a succeeding generation.'

'You've got to be joking!'

Wilbur shrugged.

'You'll see, cobber.' He turned to Pamela. 'Personally, doctor, I think I'd quite fancy the notion of sharing my tent with you . . .'

'Yuck!' said Pamela.

A loud miaow brought a smile to her face.

'Hello, Tico,' she said.

'Sometimes I wish he was the captain,' Wilbur muttered. 'I've had a bellyful of Hellyer's picturesque eccentricity . . .'

'That's dangerous talk,' Snow said with a grin. 'You'll be keel-hauled or marooned on an asteroid if you're not careful.'

'Yeah? Or maybe there'll be a mutiny and he'll be cast adrift with a cask of water and a sextant!'

Carrying a purring Tico in her arms, Pamela stepped on to the bridge. In the starshine she saw Hellyer erect behind his wheel, his eyes on the outline of the sails.

'A fair wind, cap'n?'

He smiled. She was the only one with whom he could relax.

'Don't you start. One colourful character is enough on this clipper.'

'Most of the crew think it's more than enough,' she said. 'I find morale at a dangerous low.'

'Of course.' Hellyer made an impatient gesture with his hand. 'Doctor, you're on this craft because you're a psychiatrist as well as a saw-bones. Surely you must understand . . .'

'It's hardly my place to analyse my captain, but off hand I'd say that, like others in positions of ultimate responsibility, you have an identity crisis . . .'

'We're not talking about me,' he snapped. 'Oh, it'll all fit into place.'

'Quickly I hope, or we'll all be dead of boredom before we're half way there.'

'Need some excitement do you – a shipboard drama?'

'It would help.'

'In that case, girl, switch on No 5 monitor, there's your drama.'

The big TV screen glowed and an image came into focus against a background of remote constellations. It was a ship similar to *Pioneer* except that instead of a ring of sails it had several triangular ones set at different angles to the hull.

'What on Earth's that?'

'That, my dear, is a computer image assembled from information provided by our scanners,' said Hellyer grimly. 'It's an East Bloc starclipper bound for Proxima Centuari and standing about thirty light seconds astern. In other words, the race is on for Terra Nova.'

'I don't understand.'

'The East Bloc has constructed a starclipper as similar to ours as their supersonic passenger aircraft was to Concorde. With a project as enormous as the construction of *Pioneer* there must have been at least one traitor capable of passing on specifications. I might add that this contender does not surprise me – I'd been warned of the possibility by Space Centre.'

'But what does it mean to us?'

'Only that we shall have to reach Terra Nova ahead of them, and that means – in the terminology of my great-grandfather – setting the stu'ns'ls!'

His eyes flashed with enthusiasm and his knuckles shone whitely as he gripped the spokes of the great wheel. And for the first time Pamela heard him laugh, a sound so unexpected that Tico fled with a wail of surprise.

Electronics Engineer William Davidson lay on his bunk and eyed his foam-lined ceiling sombrely. He had played his Shostakovich tapes so often that even they palled, while the videos from the clipper's library bored him with their puerile entertainment content and lack of social message. Yet when he sat in the recreation lounge he made such a pretence of enthusiasm for videos of colonialist settlers snatching territory from American Indians that he was nicknamed The Cowboy. His fellow crew members would have been astonished if they had known the man behind the mask. But they had no more inkling of his view of capitalistic society than the various boards who had evaluated his suitability for work in space. None guessed at his contacts with East Bloc representatives when on foreign holidays, nor the mission which had been entrusted to him.

In the belief that NASA would be the first to send a manned spacecraft beyond the solar system, he had been recruited as a mole who would act only when it became imperative for the protection of the East Bloc's own plans for outer space. Sooner or later he believed his time would come, but the waiting . . . the waiting while he tried to act like the rest of the shallow fools who manned the ship, subservient to a crazy dictator living on fantasies. He believed that in a democratic East Bloc ship a council of spaceworkers would make collective decisions.

At least his plans to subvert the crew were progressing. While never appearing to criticise Hellyer, he said enough to sow the seeds of dissatisfaction, especially with Wilbur Mantell who might be worked up to a pitch of mutiny.

Glancing over the side of his bunk Davidson swore. Tico was nosing about the cabin. To the engineer the Foreign Black symbolized Hellyer and all he stood for. He picked up his rare printed book, *The Decay of the West,* and was about to hurl it at the animal when the sound of an emergency chime sent him running.

Hellyer stood at the wheel under the transparent dome of the bridge, an unmoving silhouette against the galactic stardust. He sighed, feeling old and very alone.

He had outlived his comrades of the early expeditions when they had sailed like young argonauts under Saturn's eerie rings and cruised above the boiling clouds of Venus. Now there was not only a generation gap between himself and his crew, but something else – they had been trained to undertake their duties without the words 'adventure' or 'romance' in their vocabularies.

He sighed again as he recalled his briefing sessions with the psychologists who planned the *Pioneer* programme which, as a good officer, he followed to the last detail. But he knew he was out of date, a colourful relic – the old salt piloting his clipper among the stars. He turned to where the cat was cleaning his paws.

'You and me, Tico,' he said aloud, and was not quite sure what he meant.

It was time. He went to a control panel and pressed the button which filled *Pioneer* with chimes, and gruffly told a microphone that all hands were to assemble on the bridge.

For a long time the captain regarded the crew members, his faded eyes moving slowly from face to face.

'I hear there are mutterings on the mess deck,' he said in a low voice. 'I hear there is dissatisfaction over this voyage. Am I right, Mr Ryan?'

'Well, sir, none of us expected such a long mission,' the Australian answered. 'I guess we weren't prepared for it, and we're still over two light years away from Terra Nova, and well . . .' His voice trailed away.

'In my great-grandfather's day there were times when the sails of the great clippers hung limp in the doldrums,' Hellyer said. 'Times when the sea was as still as a painting, and the sun burned the skin off the crew as they lay waiting for that first faint sigh which heralded a breeze . . . '

'With respect, sir,' said Wilbur Mantell, 'we did not sign on a clipper ship.'

'With respect, Mr Mantell,' retorted the captain. 'With respect, you signed on a ship, and it matters not whether the wind that blows it be solar or Pacific trade. The fact is you signed on for a voyage into the unknown – a voyage that will rank you in history with Leif Ericsson, Columbus and Captain Cook. There is nothing you can do to alter the situation, so why not make the most of it?'

He paused dramatically.

'Here is something which will cure your lethargy.'

He switched on the monitor and the crew saw the starclipper with the triangular sails.

As Hellyer explained the race between the Free World and the East Bloc to claim territory for space colonization, he was rewarded by the growing excitement of the crew. Questions were fired at him on the speed and technical features of their pursuer, and there were mutterings against an enemy which attempted to snatch their achievement and use Terra Nova as a base to infect the universe with a de-humanizing philosophy.

When the questions had been answered, and they still stood hypnotized by the East Bloc clipper, Wilbur Mantell asked, 'What can we do about it, sir?'

'We shall extend the mast and clap on extra sails, and the solar wind will give us more speed. You have all been trained to fit spare sails in the event of meteor damage, and this will be a similar operation.'

They began to grin at this break in their routine. To get outside the ship in space suits, to work physically on the masts, and above all to feel the heady sense of contest with the ship in their wake, was exactly what they needed.

'Engineer Davidson, you will remain on the bridge to control the mast extensions,' Hellyer said. 'The rest of you will suit up and assemble at No 1 mast with the extra sail.'

Touching black Tico for luck, they departed in high spirits.

Within a terrestrial hour Captain Hellyer watched them follow-my-leader up the mast which loomed directly in front of the bridge dome. The bulky but weightless roll of carbon fibre sail floated after them at the end of a line.

Behind the captain, William Davidson sat at the control console which activated the mast mechanisms and the auxiliary yards which would telescope out to allow extra sails to be rigged. On a special panel a series of illuminated buttons glowed like ominous rubies. One for each mast, they were destruct buttons to be used in emergency – such as a meteorite strike – when it would be necessary to jettison wreckage.

'Sir, we're ready to attach the stu'ns'l,' came the voice of Snow Ryan over the sound system tuned to the crew's helmet radios.

'Excellent. As soon as you have it fast we'll raise the yards.'

'Ay, ay, cap'n.'

With his head at an uncomfortable angle Hellyer watched the carbon fibre curtain unrolled by the tiny silver figures floating round the masthead by their safety lines.

Davidson's dry tongue slid along his dry lips. Never would he get such a chance to serve his cause. At all costs the East Bloc clipper had to reach Terra Nova first!

He drew a deep breath, and found the act was much easier than he had expected. As his finger stabbed the No 1 destruct button a silent explosion illuminated the bridge briefly, and the sheared mast with a great shadow of torn sail floated away from the hull. With it went a merry-go-round of glittering dolls whirling at the end of their lines. The babel of the bewilderment – in some cases screams – filled the dome.

Hellyer turned and looked straight into the muzzle of the simple pistol which Davidson had fashioned in his workshop for just such an occasion.

'Mutiny, by hell!' the captain shouted and lunged at the engineer. Davidson fired and the slug caught Hellyer in the chest, throwing him against the wheel. The reek of crude powder filled the bridge, causing Tico to sneeze. Like a man filmed in slow motion, Hellyer grasped the wheel and, as it turned under his weight, slumped to the floor.

Davidson switched off the sound system and a merciful silence replaced the clamour of the doomed crew. For a moment he looked up and saw that the mast and the marionettes circling it were falling behind the starclipper.

'Why?' gasped Hellyer.

'The capitalistic system has done enough damage on earth without creating neo-feudal states out among the stars,' Davidson said. 'I have done my duty to mankind.'

'And murdered your comrades.'

'A small price to pay for the East Bloc clipper reaching the new planet first. I shall rendezvous with her, then *Pioneer* will be left to drift without sails – a *Marie Celeste* of space. By the time Space Centre realize that she is lost our flag will be flying on Terra Nova.'

He looked up again and saw that the debris of the mast had now drifted out of his line of vision.

A terrible sound came from the dying captain. For a moment Davidson thought it was a death rattle, then realized it was laughter.

'What, old man?' he demanded in alarm. From the pilot's chair Tico watched with wide eyes, then jumped down and rubbed against Hellyer's arm. In an automatic response his ivory fingers slid along the sleek fur.

'Lieutenant Tico, you will assume command,' he muttered.

'I always knew you were mad,' shouted Davidson.

Hellyer's laughter died as a series of shudders racked his body.

'Listen,' he gasped. 'I must tell you while I can . . . there is no East Bloc starclipper . . . What you did not understand is that this entire voyage was programmed . . . I have been merely a colourful figurehead for the crew to identify with – to provide a focal point for their frustration. There is a human aversion to taking orders from computers on long space voyages . . .'

Sweat dewed out on Davidson's forehead.

'You mean?'

'The so-called East Bloc starclipper was a fiction – a mere video image programmed to be shown at this time to help the crew over their mid-voyage tedium – to renew their enthusiasm for the project . . . In flight entertainment you might call it.' Again the ghastly chuckle.

'And without me or the crew, *Pioneer* will still land on Terra Nova . . .'

'Not with me aboard,' Davidson cried. He seized the spokes of the ship's wheel and spun it.

'Nobody can alter course,' Hellyer whispered. 'That wheel is genuine – like my great-grandfather – but here it is a theatrical prop.'

Long after Captain Hellyer died, Davidson sat slumped in the pilot's chair, his mind a cauldron of rage and despair. He had murdered for his ideal only to find he had achieved nothing except his own destruction. He would never be able to return to earth nor would he ever attend a ceremony in which a red flag was hoisted on the soil of the new world.

Finally his anger exploded into madness. Somebody, something must pay! . . . He seized the empty pistol and advanced on Tico. The cat sensed his danger and with an outraged wail fled from the bridge. Davidson followed, waving the gun like a club. Perhaps because he was the only other sentient creature on the ship, the cat became the symbol of everything the engineer hated.

The hunting of Tico became an absorbing game. The engineer stalked the cat along the endless corridors, searching cabin after cabin and sealing each so the animal could not return and hide. Yet, apart from an occasional glimpse of a black shape vanishing in the distance, his hunt was fruitless.

Then he remembered the feeding routine. At certain times the robotic food machine in the galley provided Tico with his milk and protein granules. All he would have to do was lie in wait. He went to his workshop and recharged the pistol.

Tico was hungry. He knew it was time to stroll to the place where milk would appear magically in his dish. But he was nervous of the human who had been chasing him. His feline sense of preservation told him to tread carefully.

He reached the galley threshold, and then his tail became twice its normal size as his whiskers warned that the enemy was within. With a yowl of annoyance, he ran down a corridor towards the ship's technical area.

Davidson raced after him, his pistol cocked for when the animal should pause long enough for him to take aim.

The first door Tico found open belonged to the chemistry laboratory, a place he had avoided because smells there sometimes burned the inside of his aristocratic nose. But now he ran behind tangles of glass tubing set up for an experiment which would never be completed.

His eyes turning as restlessly as radar antennae, Davidson entered and froze. Through a carboy of acid he saw the distorted shape of a black cat. He raised his pistol and fired. The bullet shattered the glass and a wave of acid poured from the shelf. Vapour rolled towards the engineer while a black shape flashed past his legs.

As the caustic mist thickened about him he turned to the exit only to see the firedoor slide across it. Delicate sensors had inhaled the fumes and the ship's safety control computer sealed the area.

William Davidson stood motionless while the vapour dissipated. It had stung his eyes, but the real reason for the hot tears glistening on his face was the knowledge that, without crew members to open the fire door from the outside, he was trapped as surely as if he had been sealed in a tomb.

On schedule *Pioneer's* computers put her into orbit above Terra Nova. Her umbrella sails retracted and, with retro-rockets roaring, she drifted down to the surface.

The hominoid population of the planet was in the neolithic stage of its development. The knowledge of metal working still lay ahead of them and their religious belief, though intense, was centred on objects of stone. This was to change when a tribe on a pilgrimage to its sacred plain heard thunder in the heavens and beheld a shining temple descend on a column of flame. They abased themselves as the temple came to rest, towering above them like a spire.

Aboard *Pioneer* circuits surged with electronic life as commands flashed from the computer banks. The airlock opened and a metal ramp lowered itself to the ground.

To the hominoids the opening of the door was a supernatural invitation to enter, and fear of disobeying it over-rode their fear of the mysterious tower. Inside they crept along metal tunnels until they reached the sanctuary of the god who had brought them this wonderful gift.

Entering the bridge they fell to their knees again when they saw a black apparition regarding them with divine green eyes. Before his throne was a scattering of sacrificial bones . . .

84

'Behold the Furred God,' cried the shaman who, like the rest of his kind, was quick to take advantage of the unexpected.

The temple of the Furred God was to provide the tribe with great wonders. The metal they plundered to make spear and arrow heads ensured that they became the paramount tribe in the region. Meanwhile their deity remained where invisible spirits provided the white liquid essential to his welfare. Sometimes he ventured down the ramp and scratched the alien soil. This was seen as a symbolic gesture of ownership, but as time passed he preferred to remain in his sanctuary.

The shaman – now high priest of the cult of the Furred God – spent much time with him. When he heard a throaty rumble come from his master he announced to the tribe he had received a sign that it was propitious to sow their crops or slaughter their neighbours.

And in gratitude the tribe honoured the Furred God by erecting a double row of megaliths on their sacred plain, each one carved in his likeness.

Arbuthnot Road

Stella Whitelaw

A senior official of the local council authority recommended that Arbuthnot Road should be demolished and its inhabitants, mostly elderly people, be rehoused. He thought it a good decision. Two years later he was in the Birthday Honours list and his wife bought a feathered hat for the presentation at Buckingham Palace.

The elderly residents of Arbuthnot Road did not go to Buckingham Palace. They were rehoused in small flats. It was argued that at their time of life they would appreciate modern heating and indoor loos. To some extent they did, but many pined for the old road and their diminutive gardens.

The bulldozers moved in and soon the area was a heap of rubble with shreds of faded brown wallpaper fluttering in the dust cloud, heavy old mantlepieces leaning drunkenly against splintered and smouldering timbers. Once the crashing of the demolition ball and collapsing brick walls had ceased, Arbuthnot Road died. The nettles grew in silence and pale pink lupins pushed their heads through the rubble from buried herbaceous borders like souls of the dead. Almost unnoticed, the new inhabitants moved in.

The first cats were not new to Arbuthnot Road. They were domestic pets abandoned because their elderly owners had been rehoused in controlled premises. These cats were shocked and withdrawn, used to living with people, they were not equipped to forage for themselves and did not understand why they had been left behind. They hung around their old haunts waiting for a miracle to restore everything to normality.

Into their nervous midst stalked a leader, a big black feral tom. He was a second generation feral and totally wild with a ferocity and cunning sharpened by a lifetime of self-defence. His mother had

86

been thrown out by a family when they realised she was pregnant. They panicked, took the queen to a rubbish tip in a cardboard box and left her. She reared her kittens in the same box, but she too was used to living with man and pined away.

The strongest of her kittens grew into a lean and lethal man-hater. He was quiet unapproachable. He had lived in dockyard factories, and marshland near a derelict airfield; he dominated any colony he joined. He fought, he hunted, he killed. He fathered dozens of scrawny wild-eyed kittens. Savagely dangerous, the tom was the nearest to a wild beast that a cat could get.

Santa, on the other hand, was a Christmas kitten, passed around in the New Year like the unwanted present he was. The last of his new owners could not cope with a kitten but were too soft-hearted to say no and too squeamish to drown him. Twice he had been half way to a bucket. Santa decided he was not going to risk a third trip. When he simply disappeared, nobody cared.

A cross-eyed tortoiseshell had quite a different background. He had been encouraged to live in an old red-brick fever hospital. Both staff and patients fed him, and many an elderly patient partially owed their recovery to the therapeutic purring which kept them company on long lonely afternoons. When the hospital was closed down due to a Government cut, no one thought of their loyal vermin catcher.

'Whatever happened to old Loopy?' one of the porters asked as he packed the last of the patient files into plastic boxes for removal. No one knew. Loopy was at that moment, roaming the empty wards, puzzled, wondering where everyone had gone. When it finally dawned on him that his source of hospital meals had also vanished, he cleared off. He wasn't catching their mice for nothing. He was a strong cat, in good condition, and drifted into the colony growing in Arbuthnot Road. But he kept out of the way of the big tom.

This lack of understanding in their changed circumstances brought on definite personality changes in the domestic cats. The sleek grey had had a long and comfortable existence with a kind and caring pensioner who had talked to him constantly. His world became melancholy and silent when the old woman suddenly died. No one remembered her cat in the excitement and bustle of the police being called in to break down the door; the welfare organised her funeral after trying to contact uninterested relations. Tibbles sat outside the smashed door for days but no one noticed him. He was just another neighbourhood cat. Eventually he gave up waiting and wandered away. He sat on the fringe of the colony because there was nothing else to do. His life might as well have been over.

The most exotic cat in the colony was Samantha. She was pert and pretty, once a valuable Cream Persian. She had been abandoned when her owners booked a holiday in Barbados and had then found out about the boarding charges at a cattery.

'We need this holiday more than we need the cat,' they argued among themselves, shrill and guilt laden.

They threw her out of the car window on the way to Heathrow. She crouched, dazed, on the hard shoulder of the motorway until sheer hunger forced her to find food. After the big tom mated with her, she followed him like some kind of groupie.

Another, kinder family did take Jupiter, their seal point Siamese, with them to their new home, but they never ensured that he became familiar with his new surroundings before they let him out. They had so many things to think about. Jupiter was full of curiosity, went for a stroll and got lost; he wandered for miles with increasing confusion, unable to find anyone or anything that was recognisable. Eventually he reached what was left of Arbuthnot Road. The family put an ad in the paper but, of course, Jupiter could not read.

Nor were all the cats fierce. Thomas, a thin tabby, had spent a terrified kittenhood with a noisy and undisciplined family where the children pulled his tail, tied his paws with string and shot caps into his face. One day the husband left home. The next day Thomas did the same. It was the bravest thing he ever did. Everyone cried, but whether it was for the cat or the father, no one was a hundred per cent sure.

The Arbuthnot Road colony grew as the toms and queens mated and bred. The kittens were very wild and could not be touched. Some of the cats remembered their domesticated lives and would occasionally accept food from a quiet middle-aged woman who always took a short cut through the waste ground to her job at a supermarket. She began saving scraps of stale cheese, bacon and old bread. Sometimes there was a bit of mouldy ham.

'Here, here, here,' she called to the distant cats watching her from piles of broken bricks. The site had never been properly cleared. 'Puss, puss, puss.'

The ferals did not move. They had forgotten the meaning of puss, puss, puss, if they had even ever known it. But they did know that humans had a diminished sense of responsibility towards them. The drunks trod on them, swore and threw bottles. Youths chased them with beer cans and bricks. A clutch of kittens had simply disappeared when the site had been invaded by a swarm of school thugs with penknives and wire and boxes of matches. So the ferals were not moving for anyone.

'Puss, puss, puss,' the woman persisted. She was not called Martha Strong for nothing. She lived a street away from Arbuthnot Road. The demolition squad had stopped short of her house, though the work had not helped her outer wall and now it was shored up with timber.

Tibbles was the first to move, stretching his thin grey body as he walked nonchalantly towards her as if actually intending to go the other way. She was holding out a handful of cheese. He had once adored cheese. His mistress had always shared a cheese sandwich with him at bedtime.

'Full of protein,' she used to say. 'I'll never starve as long as I can buy a bit of cheese . . .' She little knew that cheese would not save her from falling out of bed and lying on the floor with a broken hip until dehydration and a heart attack finished her off.

Tibbles gulped down a few scraps of cheese, then bolted for cover. He did not trust her. Samantha darted forward, judging that she might as well have a piece of the action.

'Wicked shame,' said Martha, crumbling a bit of cheese for the dirty white cat. 'I reckon you could do with a good bath. Not much of a little beauty now, are you?'

The other cats stayed like statues. Santa watched the woman with narrowed green eyes. He knew she had food and he was hungry. She had a shopping bag that looked a bit like a bucket. He dared not risk it.

Martha straightened up and scattered the cheese on the ground. She supposed they did not mind a bit of dirt with it. As soon as she was out of sight, the cats swarmed on the cheese, biting and scratching for the scraps. The big tom snatched the biggest chunk and growled at anyone who dared to challenge him for it. He slunk back to his domain inside a crushed water tank and chewed carefully. No one knew that his teeth were rotten and there was not much he could eat these days. His size and strength still made him the leader, but if he could not eat he would grow weak. There were several younger cats, lean and wild-eyed, waiting to take his place.

It began to rain. The cats shook themselves and ran to find shelter among the rubble. Thomas stayed out in the rain, sniffing among the earth to find sodden fragments of cheese left by the others. It was the only way he fed. He was so timid. The rain plastered his fur to his thin ribs; he was starving and looked it.

'Has it ever stopped raining this summer?' asked Inspector Alan Murphy, turning from the window to accept a cup of tea from Celia Hamilton, the young veterinary surgeon who had recently joined the league. She was a very business-like young woman with over-sized glasses and a severe haircut. It looked as if she cut it herself, unless the urchin look was high fashion.

'I don't believe it has,' she said briefly.

'Settle down everyone,' said Mrs MacKay, chairman of the league's working party. 'We've got a lot to get through. And this month we must decide what we are going to do about the Arbuthnot Road colony.'

'More complaints?'

'Dozens of them. Apart from the general nuisance of smells and dead cats, they are beginning to invade nearby houses for food. They knock over milk bottles, steal from kitchen tables, dig up gardens. It has become a very large colony and no one dares to leave a baby outside in a pram.'

'A cat wouldn't attack a baby, surely?' asked Celia.

'It's the milk around a baby's mouth that attracts the cat,' said Alan Murphy. 'The baby could get scratched.'

'Sounds like a horror film,' she shuddered.

'We must consider all the methods open to us,' said Mrs MacKay. She was a round little woman, almost cat-like in appearance, and she had spent thirty years working for animal welfare. It had begun with a small rescue centre for strays which she had run single-handed. Now she was in demand for committee work of various kinds, and she sometimes thought the paperwork exceeded the practical. She had so little time for looking after her own cats.

It was not a new situation for the league by any means. There were some 12,000 cats living wild in the 704 colonies which had been located in Great Britain. People did not believe Mrs MacKay when she told them the statistics. And obviously there were a lot more colonies undetected. It could mean a feral population of perhaps a quarter million.

Hospitals were a favourite spot for colonies to establish themselves, hidden in the heating plant, closely followed by factories and dockyards. Cats attached themselves to military camps, schools, caravan sites, rubbish tips, power stations, farms and prisons. They were not all a nuisance. As from their earliest history in Egypt, they were valued for keeping down rodents. In this way they were unlike many other species of wild animals, and it was for this reason that the league had developed different methods of containing a colony.

'There are several courses of action open to us,' she began, chiding herself for sounding like a trade unionist. These were real creatures whose fate they were deciding, brave and fierce, living as best they could in a foreign environment.

'Firstly, we could leave the colony alone and allow nature to take its course. That is, the survival of the fittest.'

'More dead and bedraggled cats.'

'Secondly, the complete eradication of the colony by trapping and killing.' To her own ears, she now sounded like a concentration camp commander.

'A bit drastic.'

'Sometimes if a colony has lost its source of food, say an old hospital has closed, then it is the most humane course. But in the case of Arbuthnot Road, probably another colony would form and we would have to do it all over again.'

'No, thank you,' said Celia, knowing who would have to do the wholesale killing.

'We could reduce the numbers by controlled culling, trapping and re-housing any suitable cats. This is the cheapest method but the result is not a permanent solution.'

'Fourthly, we could trap the entire colony, neuter and return to site. This does stabilize the life of the colony and improve general

91

health. Or lastly we could try chemical birth control. Of these last two methods, we must consider the cost of such operations. Perhaps the local authority could be persuaded to fork up some money . . .'

The working party talked far into the afternoon about the future of the cats living in Arbuthnot Road. Inspector Murphy watched their new recruit with veiled interest. That brisk, no nonsense manner was hiding a rather insecure young woman, he decided.

Celia contributed only the briefest remarks to the discussion. She was frozen with fear. Suddenly she had forgotten everything she had learned at veterinary college; supposing she could not manage the sterilizations, the trappings, the injections, the euthanasias?

Alan Murphy leaned across the table. 'You won't have to do everything by yourself,' he assured her. 'You will have help.'

'Thanks,' she said. She was not sure whether he was laughing at her or not. She was unused to men, that's why she worked with animals. She turned away so that he could not see her face.

As the rain stopped, the cats came out to dry themselves. They were a matted and bedraggled lot with torn ears and eye infections. Some made valiant efforts to clean up. The really wild ones, although they had a cat's inborn habits, were less compulsive. There was too much fighting and foraging to be done. Grooming was way down on the list of priorities.

Two people came to the site and began walking about in wellington boots and climbing over the rubble with notebooks. The cats watched from afar. They knew nothing about the working party's decision.

'Trying to count ferals is impossible,' said Alan, helping Celia over a dangerous pile of planking. 'One is never quite sure, unless the marking is very distinctive. The same cat can get listed twice – or more.'

'There's no mistaking that big black tom, a ferocious looking brute, or that grubby white persian. I bet that's an abandoned pet. She's hardly chocolate box prettiness now, more like a squashed box of liquorice allsorts,' said Celia. She was feeling less of a new girl now that she was out of the meeting and on site.

'That sad looking grey might be quite friendly. See how he's watching our every movement while pretending to be quite disinterested. Rustle your paper bag and see what happens.'

'Yes, a definite twitch of the ears,' said Celia, amused. 'He's wondering if I've brought any goodies. Urgh, look at all this mouldy sliced bread. No wonder they get infected.'

They put down several dishes of food and retired to a distance to watch the behaviour of the colony. As they thought, the tamest ventured out first, but they were then quickly followed by the wild ones. It turned into a snarling scrap for every morsel, sharp teeth ready to snatch food right out of another's mouth.

'Look at that timid tabby, right out on the fringe. It's starving. You can see it never gets anything.'

'I suppose you are going to try and feed it separately, said Alan, reading her mind. 'You're a softie.'

'Perhaps. I'm going to have a go.'

She followed Thomas across the waste ground, inch by inch, calling encouragingly, isolating him from the main group of ferals. He was a pathetic sight with ribs showing through his short muddy coat. The first candidate for the humane injection, thought Celia, trying to be dispassionate.

She herded him further away so that the other cats were not within smelling distance of the food she was going to put down for him. She scraped out the last of the fish and put the dish among some tall couch grass which would give the timid cat some cover. She then placed herself between the main colony and the food.

Thomas sat watching these manoeuvres from the safety of a derelict pram. He was curious, but too frightened to move; he knew there was food. The smell was driving him insane. He forgot about the woman crouched some yards away.

He darted forward on shaky limbs, half expecting to be set upon by the black tom, or some of the other wild cats. But none came. He reached the fish in total disbelief. It was real fish, such as he had not tasted for many mouths. He gulped the food, swallowing flakes and skin without even masticating.

'Hold on,' Celia murmured. 'You'll choke.'

The fish was demolished in seconds. Thomas had a vaguely mesmerised look. He licked every wet shred from the dish, pushing it along the ground, determined that not even the smell would escape. It was then that Thomas saved himself from the humane injection. He began to purr, quite unconsciously, as he pursued the dish through the grass.

Celia wrote down a careful description of the tabby's markings. She would find this one a home.

By the end of the week Alan and Celia had identified a fair number of the cats and noted their condition. They had also met Martha Strong with her bag from the supermarket.

'Oh no, I couldn't possibly have a cat,' she said, alarmed and defensive. 'I'm out all day and the price of cat food is awful.'

'But you're managing to feed several cats now on the scraps you collect,' said Celia persuasively.

'But if it were my own cat, that would be different. I'd have to buy the food. Then there's the milk. I can't afford a pint of fresh any more. Anyway I wouldn't fancy one of these cats. They're full of fleas.'

'We'd make sure the cat was in perfect condition before it came to you. No fleas,' said Celia. 'And sterilized.'

A van appeared near the site. The men began to unload wood and wire traps. It was essential to trap the females first, and with Martha's help they had been able to pick out those cats she had seen pregnant or with kittens. For a few days a dummy trap was left on the site with food inside, so that the cats became used to it. The trap was padlocked to a rusty hulk of iron. Traps were often stolen. They made good rabbit hutches.

Alan decided to use a manual trap rather than the automatic type, even though it meant a long patient wait for the operator, but he could be selective. It was no use trapping a bold tom, if the pregnant female he really wanted was sitting inches away. Once the trap door had sprung, the female would be too nervous to come near it for weeks, if ever again.

The traps were mainly wood which cats preferred, with an open view all round. Inside were wire modules which could convert the trap into a crush cage so that Celia could work on a cat without being bitten or scratched.

Alan sat in the van, half reading a newspaper. The cord from the trap came through the window and was looped to the door handle. He had sandwiches and a thermos of coffee. He was prepared for a long wait.

94

He watched the plump white persian. She was definitely with kitten. She was filthy, scratching herself to distraction. Alan longed to use a very effective spray and solve one of her miseries.

He unwrapped his substantial sandwiches, ham, egg, cheese, lettuce and tomato. Being a bachelor, he believed in good plain food. That young Celia, now, she needed feeding up.

'I'll make her a Dagwood sandwich one day,' he chuckled.

They were soon to receive a batch of automatic traps that had spring loaded drop bars to secure the door. These could be put out, baited and left. Alan was not so keen on them. It was difficult to remove a cat from these without it escaping, and it was not possible to comb the cat to the end for an injection. The trap could be vandalized, with or without a cat in it. They were, however, inexpensive, and that today was a prime consideration.

Samantha was the first to be caught, beguiled by the bait of squashed minced chicken. Alan pulled up the slack cord, then went towards the trap, keeping it absolutely taut. Samantha flew into a temper when she realised she was caught, hurling herself at the sturdily welded steel mesh sides. Alan bolted the door, put the paddle down the centre slit and gently pushed her to one side so that she might settle down. She tried to evade the paddle by squeezing herself over the top of it.

'It's no use you trying to do that,' Alan soothed, tossing in a few crunchy cat biscuits. 'Now then, calm down.'

Samantha crouched at the back of the cage, spitting and hissing. She had once been addicted to cat biscuits, but they had been out of her diet so long she had almost forgotten them. The factory-made shapes slid under her paws as Alan loaded the trap into the van. She pounced and crunched.

Back at the clinic, Celia's routine was an anaesthetic injection, followed by the sterilization operation. Then the cat was injected with a long acting antibiotic and checked for fleas and mites. But as Samantha was heavily pregnant Celia decided to wait until the kittens were born. Meanwhile her coat was treated while she was still trapped by the paddle. Celia reached for the spray canister.

'This cat's absolutely crawling,' she said with a shudder as the fleas hopped out onto her sleeve. 'And her ears are infected where she's scratched like mad. Some people might say that a jab of

95

phentobarbitone sodium would be more sensible.'

'But not you,' said Alan from the outer unit where he was disinfecting the trap before re-use. 'In a couple of days, she'll be a little beauty. We ought to try and find her a home.'

'You try,' said Celia. 'We'll have to keep her a few weeks because of the kittens.'

Tibbles, the melancholy grey, was the next to be caught. He walked right into it. He had always had a passion for boxes, baskets and sitting in paper bags. After sterilization and a thorough wash and brush up, he was returned to the site faintly bemused and dozy.

That evening Martha came along with her usual bag of goodies. She put her shopping basket on the ground and without thinking Tibbles got in and curled round on top of her library book and the evening newspaper, and went to sleep.

It seemed like an omen. Martha scuttled home, looking guiltily behind her. It seemed almost like stealing. Once in the seclusion of her small kitchen, she put down the basket and poured out a saucer of milk. Tibbles opened one eye.

'It's only dried,' she said apologetically. 'But a lot of people can't tell the difference. Of course, I could bring home a carton of fresh milk from the supermarket, now that there's the two of us. After all, it wouldn't go to waste. That is, if you decide to stay.'

Three days later Tibbles jumped onto her lap. As Martha slowly stroked his bony head, she felt almost happy. Tibbles was wondering if she knew how to make a cheese sandwich. He would take a chance on her breaking a hip.

The trapping went on slowly and cautiously. It was work that could not be hurried. But the big tom escaped all capture. He would dart into a trap, snatch the bait and be out again before the door could be shut. Alan swore to himself, mildly, as the big cat leaped over the rubble and disappeared from sight.

Gradually all the other cats were caught, sterilized, treated for fleas and their ears nicked for identification. A few old and diseased cats were put down. Celia hated doing this. She leaned against the table, feeling quite faint. The dead cat was a pathetic sight, mangy and sick. Alan saw how pale she was and quietly put the body into a plastic bag for incineration.

'Found a home for the white one yet?' he asked, changing the subject, though he knew quite well it was still being housed at the clinic. 'I see she's had her kittens.'

'Why ask me?' said Celia, sharper than she meant to be. 'I'm not a welfare officer. Why don't you have her yourself if you are so keen.'

'If I gave a home to every cat I liked, I'd be over-run with the creatures,' he said cheerfully. He was so much older than Celia, ordinary and uninteresting, he knew there was nothing he could do but keep his growing affection for her at a distance. It pleased him to help her in little ways, knowing the long hours she worked and the serious attitude she took towards her work. Those big glasses and severe haircut made her look plain, but to Alan she was just a scared young woman, trying to be grown up.

'I haven't seen the timid tabby come in yet,' said Celia, plunging her arms deep in hot soapy water. She was aware she had been short with Alan, and he was always so kind. 'Do you know the one I mean? The one that never gets any food.'

'I haven't seen it around lately. We've just the big tom to get now and we can call it a day at Arbuthnot Road. The new automatic traps have arrived so we could put a couple of those out and move onto the next job.'

'I'll put them on the site if you're busy elsewhere. I'd like a breath of air.'

Celia wanted to find out for herself what had happened to the timid tabby. She did not like the thought of the cat being holed up somewhere, perhaps injured or ill. She took some chloroform with her, just in case. She had to be prepared to give it a whiff straight away if it was beyond help.

As she parked her car at the lower end of Arbuthnot Road, she saw a movement of cats disappearing. And even that brief glimpse confirmed that the ferals were generally in better health. Stabilization of their numbers always seemed to have this effect.

Celia put a new automatic reinforced wire mesh cage in place and spread some strong smelling pilchards for bait. The hinged door had a release mechanism which dropped when the cat stepped on a contact plate at the rear of the trap.

She scrambled over the rubble, glad to be away from the clinic for an hour, to relax away from the responsibility of the work. Mrs MacKay and the committee were watching her all the time, evaluating her competence. Even Alan kept an eye on her. It was like working in a glass bowl.

She turned over unspeakable rubbish with a stick knowing that the tabby might be hiding in a very small place, too frightened to come out and look for food. She had saved some pilchards though she really expected to find it dead somewhere.

Thomas watched her from the depths of a rusty drain pipe. He had been alarmed by all the recent activity on the site. His eyes glinted moistly in the darkness. He was so thin he had no trouble squeezing himself down to the end of the pipe and then turning. He was shaking with nerves though he knew no one could see him.

Celia moved on, a tall grey figure on a grey afternoon, and soon she was out of sight. Thomas tucked his nose into what was left of his fur and tried to sleep, but the muscles of his hollow stomach gnawed and cramped. Sleep was impossible. It was a life beyond hope for Thomas. He thought of nothing.

After half an hour of searching, Celia gave up. He must be dead. She strolled back to her car, hands deep in her pockets, fingering the phial of chloroform.

Suddenly a piercing scream split the air. It was the most horrifying sound Celia had ever heard. She ran towards the unearthly shrieks. No human could make that cry . . .

The big tom had tried his trick again. But the new cage was much narrower than the old wooden manual type. He could not streak in and streak out without turning round, and in turning he had touched the contact plate and released the rod. He moved fast but so did the mechanism.

He was outside the cage, a writhing, seething, snarling black mass of animal fury, his back leg and tail trapped by the door. As he struggled to pull his foot free, so the weight of the door pulled closer. The bone was showing through the torn flesh and blood.

Celia was shocked and appalled. The tom was outside the cage so she could not use the grasper even if she could get it in through the small hatch. This tom, quite apart from being the wildest of the bunch, was incensed with pain. It was quite unapproachable, but then she could not leave it in pain while she went for help. She had to do something; there was the chloroform.

She took off her raincoat, intending to wrap it tightly round all that spitting, clawing hatred. Then she might be able to sprinkle some chloroform on a pad and put the cat out long enough to release the foot, push the creature back into the cage and secure the door with the drop bar. It might just work.

But she was dealing with 20 lbs of crazed wild animal. The big tom had years of fighting for his life behind him. The slim young vet, fresh from college, was no match for him. He sank his teeth and claws into her raincoat, ripping it out of her hands. A long scratch opened up on her forearm, welling pricks of red. As she reached for her coat, he leaped on her. She fell awkwardly, the phial of chloroform flew from her grasp and smashed on a brick. The cat was clinging to her legs, claws ripping her stockings and sinking into the soft flesh. She fought off the snarling teeth with her bare hands, gasping, trying to shield her face. She rolled back as the fumes from the chloroform started her coughing. She tried to crawl away, but the cat hung on. She was dragging the cat and the trap . . . the last thing she remembered as she passed out was that the cat's teeth were bad and her wounds would be infected . . .

It was Alan who found her. He would have driven passed her parked car if he had not noticed Thomas sitting by what looked like a pile of rags. He remembered that Celia had been asking about the timid cat.

She was lying unconscious, her face and hands and legs a mass of deep scratches. Thomas was sitting on her raincoat, licking the last of the pilchard from a torn pocket. He had not been afraid when he saw that she did not move or make a sound. But now as Alan approached, he fled into the undergrowth like the small ghost he was.

Alan lifted Celia gently and she moaned against his shoulder.

'Dear God,' he said. 'What a mess.'

Her glasses were broken and he removed them; her hair was matted with dirt and blood; her blouse was torn open and he saw that round her throat she wore a thin gold chain with a small heart-shaped pendant. It looked old as if it had belonged to a mother or grandmother.

His heart was moved with love and compassion and he bent and kissed the cold metal in the soft warm hollow of her throat. He felt he was entitled to one kiss in his life, to treasure the touch and smell of her skin. Even now he did not think of her lips as being for a man like him.

She was trying to say something, her mouth moving feebly. He put his head closer and caught the word ' . . . rabies . . .'

'Don't worry, darling,' he said. 'I'm taking you to a hospital.'

She seemed to smile and then slip away again into unconsciousness. He carried her to his car.

Alan went back in the evening and found where the black tom had dragged himself and the trap. The cat's foot was almost severed, and the feral was exhausted from fighting this ruthless steel foe. But his eyes were still blazing as Alan prepared a final injection.

When the Arbuthnot Road colony was considered sterilized, Martha was persuaded to monitor their welfare. She formed, with much hesitation, a cat committee which met regularly in her front room for coffee and biscuits to discuss the feeding rota and fund raising events. She enjoyed these meetings, making friends, with Tibbles sitting on her lap purring like a motorbike.

'This is one of them,' she would say proudly. 'You wouldn't think so now, would you, to look at him?'

Finding a home for Samantha, the white persian, proved difficult. She quite refused to be separated from her kittens and they grew into a large, playful, unmanageable family. One day a black postman and his wife came into the clinic. They wanted kittens for each of their children. They fell for the pure white cat and her brood. The black family came from Barbados. They thought she was really something and called her Sugar Ray.

Thomas did not have to be caught. When Celia came out of hospital she went back to the site and found him, so weak, that she could just pick him up. For several days she fed him baby cereal from the tip of her finger and milk from a dropper. She knew she was going to keep him; she reckoned she owed him her life. The first time that he came to her, timidly but of his own accord, was a moment of joy.

'I believe he had been trying to make up his mind for days,' Celia told Alan, 'but he just didn't have the courage. I can't describe how touching it was, Alan. It was such a tremendous step for him. The first time he believed in himself enough to trust another person.'

'I think I know how he felt,' said Alan, but he did not elaborate.

Perhaps, like Thomas, one day there would come a time when he would take the same step, when he believed enough in himself to go to Celia with what was in his heart.

In the meantime there was work, their mutual concern for cats, companionship and friendship. And as he watched Celia talking to her timid little tabby, scratching the angular furry chin, he was content to wait.

Gershwin

Judy Gardiner

Laddy Silver sat looking out of the window and thinking that next year he would be seventy. The idea struck him as preposterous. He didn't look old, neither did he feel it except for a tendency towards heartburn when he stooped. Then it occurred to him that it wasn't people who changed so much as the things they did. Once he had been a dance band leader, Laddy Silver and his Syncopated Rhythm, playing at the Savoy, the Dorchester, the Trocadero and once at Buckingham Palace at a private supper party. And he was still capable of running a band if anyone wanted him to. He was a good tenor sax-player, musical arranger and businessman, but no-body wanted dance bands any more because nobody wanted to dance. At least not properly.

So Laddy lived a life of enforced retirement in a block of flats in North Finchley with his wife Dolly. And Dolly hadn't changed either, except to become a little fatter and a little more disparaging. They had met when she auditioned as a girl vocalist, and they still had the record she made of *Two Dreams Met* in a very young voice with a throb in it. But he hadn't let her sing any more after they were married because it would have been bad for her status as Mrs Laddy Silver.

He looked across at her now, on this long sunny afternoon filled with nothing but thoughts and the prospect of a cup of tea and a slice of chocolate torte at four o'clock. She was lying back in her chair with her shoes off and her mouth slightly open, and one hand was curved protectively round Gershwin, their cat.

'Gershhh . . .' whispered Laddy, forming his lips into a funnel. The cat opened lazy eyes and regarded him speculatively for a moment before going back to sleep.

'Who's Daddy's lovely boy then, eh? Daddy's lovely big boy, are we? . . .' His whispering seemed to float on the air and he watched it tickle at Gershwin's ears with a beady satisfaction. 'Coming for a little walkies, Gersh?'

'Why don't you shut up?' mumbled Dolly without opening her eyes. The hand that was round Gershwin moved upwards and began to rub the area around his neck with a drowsy expertise.

'He oughtn't to sleep so much,' Laddy complained. 'He's a fine strong cat and he ought to get about more.'

He turned his attention to the window, craning down to see into the garden. 'Here comes little Miss Whatsit. She's got a string bag full of shopping – looks like mainly vegetables.'

'Go and put the kettle on.'

'Which could be why she's so thin. Vegetables don't give you an ounce of fat, they just pass straight through.'

He went out to the kitchen, which was as warm and torpid as the lounge. A lone fly buzzed on the window. He made the tea, then stacked the tray with cups and saucers, milk and sugar and two plates each containing a hefty slice of chocolate torte.

Dolly was awake now and pushing her flimsy silver pink curls back into position. She gave Laddy a calm, distant look.

'Got his as well?'

Without replying Laddy placed the saucer of milk on the carpet between them, then bent down and stirred half a teaspoonful of sugar into it. Dolly poured the tea, and they drank it in silence while Gershwin strolled over to his saucer and inspected its contents with care.

'There's been a train disaster in Canada,' Dolly said through a mouthful of torte. 'But I don't think it's anywhere near Joe.'

'Canada's a big place,' Laddy said.

'Joe's thirty-five.'

'Thirty-six on the 5th of September.'

'I know when my own son's birthday is.'

'He's my son too.'

'We must remember to send him a card this year . . .'

Gershwin finished his milk and wiped round the saucer with his tongue. He washed his hands and face then went over to Laddy and jumped on his lap.

'Where's Daddy's lovely boy, eh? Go little walkies, shall we?'

'I wonder if Joe's got a girl,' Dolly said. Then added sharply: 'Don't hold him upside down when he's full of milk.'

'He's not upside down. He's just lying on his back in my arms.'

'For an animal to lie on its back *is* being upside down to *it*,' Dolly said, and although Laddy continued to rub Gershwin under the chin for a few moments longer, he restored him to an upright position.

'More tea?'

'No thanks.'

Conversation died.

Between the block of flats and its driveway there was a wide strip of garden which had been planted with grass, roses, and some silver birches. Considering that the North Circular was only round the corner, the sound of traffic was minimal.

Having walked as far as the garages at the back of the flats, Laddy turned and began to pace back again, pausing every now and then for Gershwin to stare at whatever caught his attention.

'It must take a lot of patience to train a cat to a collar and lead,' said a voice, and Laddy recognized little Miss Whatsit, who lived somewhere on the fourth floor. Seen close to, she had a fresh-skinned face with a bright, rather artless expression, and her age was probably no more than twenty. He noticed that she had changed her dress for a pair of jeans and that she was carrying a magazine. They had never spoken before, only smiled.

'It depends on the cat,' Laddy said. 'This one's very intelligent.'

She bent down and held out her fingers to Gershwin, who sniffed them courteously before turning away.

'If animals can't adapt to an urban society they're doomed.'

'You could say the same for humans,' Laddy said. 'If you brought Queen Victoria back she'd choke to death on diesel fumes within a couple of hours.'

'Not if she was at Balmoral,' the girl said. Then added: 'What's your cat's name?'

'Gershwin. After my favourite composer.'

'I like Tchaikovsky,' she said, 'but you couldn't call a cat that, could you?'

'Don't see why not,' Laddy replied, and wished she would go

away. To discourage her he sat down on one of the garden seats and stared hard at a bed of roses, but she sat down beside him, riffling the pages of her magazine.

'I work at the Maudesley Hospital,' she said, 'and I finish at three every afternoon this week.'

'That's nice,' he murmured, and couldn't be bothered to ask what sort of work she did. Or even to ask what her name was. It struck him that he had grown to prefer Gershwin's company to that of almost everyone else.

'I'm a physiotherapist,' she said.

'Uh-huh . . .'

Having examined the four legs of the seat with scrupulous care, Gershwin sprang lightly on to Laddy's lap and began butting his head gently against his hand. Late sunlight smiled in his eyes.

The girl opened her magazine and began to study a knitting pattern, then her attention wandered and she sat watching Laddy's hand caressing Gershwin's ears with an easy rhythm.

'Have you got any children, Mr er – ?'

'A son called Joe who lives in Canada. And the name's Laddy Silver.'

He didn't expect it to mean anything to her, not at her age. With every year that passed, fewer and fewer people betrayed any sign of recognition when his name was mentioned. Nevertheless something made him add: 'At one time I had a dance band.'

She closed her magazine and sat looking at him with unashamed curiosity.

'How interesting. My grandad once had a letter from Roy Fox.'

'Did he,' said Laddy on a falling note. Not wishing to hear any more he uncoiled Gershwin's lead, set him on his feet and led him back home. Going up in the lift to the first floor he wondered whether the girl knew that Roy Fox had been dead for quite a while.

'Nice to talk to, is she?' asked Dolly, who was in the kitchen mashing Gershwin's boiled fish with a fork.

'Who?'

'Little Miss Whatsit.'

Several answers came to mind. *About on a level with you,* was one of them, but it seemed that she didn't expect him to reply because she began calling Gershwin to come for his supper.

And that was it: Gershwin never needed calling for supper, especially when the scent of boiled fish tinted the atmosphere. He was always present and correct, weaving a vigilant arabesque in and out of her feet and exhorting her to hurry in his high eunuch miaow.

But not this evening. Without speaking they hurried through the flat – the lounge, the bedroom and the bathroom, but there was no sign of him. Only the pingpong ball by the coffee table and a round flattened patch on Laddy's bathrobe, where he sometimes liked to sleep for a change.

'Gershwin! . . . Gershie, *Gershie!* – '

Simultaneously they arrived at the open front door, open no more than a couple of inches. They glared at one another with hate.

'You didn't close it when you brought him back – '

'Look – ' Laddy said, darting back to the lounge to seize the freshly-folded evening paper. 'You opened the door to the newsboy while I was in the john – '

'I didn't – that was last night – '

Frantically they tried to disentangle one uneventful evening from another. Sometimes one of them opened the door to the newsboy and other times he shoved the paper through the letterbox.

'Never mind – it doesn't *matter!*'

Without waiting for the lift Laddy sped downstairs with Dolly scuttling rapidly behind him. They flung themselves through the big swing doors that gave onto the drive, and there was a moment of summer evening sweetness with even a blackbird singing before the squeal of tyres and the slam of a car door. And the silence that followed was total. Even the blackbird stopped in mid-phrase.

The car was a blue Renault and the man had come to a party in flat 63. He got up from his knees in front of the car holding Gershwin in his hands like a little fur rug.

'I didn't stand a chance . . .' Although he was a large man he sounded like a shocked child. 'I'd slowed right down but he ran straight under the front wheels . . .'

Ashen-faced, Laddy took Gershwin on his outstretched arms and stumbled away, conscious that Dolly was gasping and trying to touch the motionless body.

Without saying anything to the man, or to one another, they took

106

him back to the flat and laid him tenderly on the kitchen table. There was no movement, no sound. He looked as if he were asleep except that his eyes – their habitual vivid green – were still half-open.

'Gershie . . . Oh, little Gershie . . .'

'Get the vet – ring the vet – '

'What've they done to you, little baby?'

No movement, no sound. A soft, still-warm body encased in sleek fur. Helplessly Laddy groped between the front paws for the heart but couldn't find it.

'The kiss of life! – ' Dolly tried to insert a trembling red-nailed finger between the jaws, then bent her head and blew explosively into the neat little pink nostrils. Dazed as he was, it struck Laddy as a ludicrous thing to do.

'Don't,' he rasped. 'Can't you see he's already gone?'

She gave a deep choking sob and they stood shoulder to shoulder, watching the light fade from the green silver of Gershwin's eyes. It was like watching night fall.

'He's really died,' Dolly said in a disbelieving croak, and although the tears were running down their cheeks it was a terrible effort to move, or even to think.

'Come on,' Laddy managed to say finally, and blunderingly dried Dolly's face with the tea towel that hung on the airer. It was the first physical contact between them since Christmas, when he had kissed her on the ear and given her a bottle of bath oil. Passively she allowed him to lead her back into the lounge, and even attempted to swallow a little brandy when he pressed the glass to her lips.

'He's dead. One minute he was alive and now he's dead,' she intoned like a woman in a trance.

'I can't take it in,' Laddy said brokenly. 'It'll be years before I can really take it in . . .'

They had two brandies each before they were able to go back to the kitchen, steeling themselves to face the horror of Gershwin lying dead on the table. But there he was, and the coldness of death was already overtaking the warm supple beauty around which had been built two private, middle-aged worlds.

Dolly wanted to have him buried under one of the silver birches

107

down in the garden and became furiously indignant when permission was witheld on the pretext that if everyone in the flats wanted a pet interred in the garden it would cause a health hazard. Then they learned that in Golders Green there was an animal cemetery where Gershwin could be laid to rest in a plot reserved especially for cats, with dogs buried at a discreet distance away and the more non-conformist creatures such as guinea pigs and parrots planted in a corner by the entrance gate.

The foam-quilted box cost them £15 and the little headstone with his name engraved on it another £25 (cheques made payable to Elysian Fields Ltd), but at least it was somewhere peaceful and beautiful and the thought of it brought them comfort.

Returning home from the funeral they found themselves confronted by Gershwin's basket, his collar and lead and his plate and saucer. The basket they hid away, but the empty space it left was so poignant that they brought it out again, even though they avoided looking at it.

'It's all so empty without him.'

'You've still got me,' Laddy said, attempting a joke. They sat looking at one another dubiously.

At tea-time Laddy went out to the kitchen and prepared the tray, wincing when his hand automatically reached for Gershwin's saucer. He cut two large slices of apple cake.

'They said we can go back there any time we like,' Dolly said. She was sitting in her chair with her shoes kicked off. 'They said they like to feel that people go back there any time they want to be with their – their little . . .' Her eyes filled.

'We'll visit him once a week,' Laddy said. 'Twice, if you like.'

Sniffing, she poured the tea, and they both sat staring at the floor between them where Gershwin's saucer was normally placed. They wondered what they were going to do with the rest of their lives.

'A lot of people from the flats have stopped me and said how sorry they were to hear about him. They all said how much they'll miss seeing him go for his little walk in the garden with me.'

'I used to take him sometimes,' Dolly said. 'I used to love taking him for a little walk whenever you'd let me.'

'I never stopped you. You always said you couldn't walk because of your feet.'

'I've got very high insteps.'

'Drink your tea,' he said. 'And eat your cake.'

She tried to, then pushed them aside. 'I can't. I feel I'd choke.'

During the silence that ensued Laddy turned and looked out of the window. The silver birches were swaying in a soft breeze.

'We've got to pull ourselves together,' he said finally. 'The show's still got to go on.'

'Sounds like the old days,' Dolly said tonelessly. 'Broken-hearted clowns, and all that.'

'Which reminds me of a slow foxtrot,' Laddy said, and began to hum in a quavering, experimental way.

'Eat your cake and drink your tea.'

'I can't,' he said. 'I can't, any more than you can.'

'Well, stop making that stupid noise.'

The next silence lasted for five minutes and was only broken by the creak of Laddy's kneecap as he got up from his chair. He went over to the cocktail cabinet and returned with the bottle of brandy and two glasses.

'What's that for?'

'Us. If we can't face tea, we'd better find a substitute.'

Dolly looked doubtful. 'That's what we had on the day – on the day –'

'He died. Yes, I know.' Laddy poured two tots and passed one across to her. 'Drink up. It's just to help us over the worst.'

They sat listening to the distant murmur of the North Circular.

'I had a rabbit when I was a little girl,' Dolly said in a calmer voice. 'But the dog next door got it.'

'That was awful,' Laddy studied her with sudden attention. 'Didn't your Dad complain?'

'He couldn't. He was away.'

'He was away a lot, wasn't he?'

'That's how it is with commercial travellers.'

'Ah, yes,' said Laddy. 'Mine was a gents' outfitter and he had his busy times, too. Just before Ascot he never slept at all.'

'You're talking as if I never met him. I met him at our wedding and when Joe was christened, only I don't think he liked me.'

'He liked you very much.'

'I sometimes get the feeling that nobody likes me very much.'

'I like you,' Laddy said. Then gave a heavy sigh when he remembered that this was the time of day when he always took Gershwin for a walk.

As there was no point in going on his own he poured another brandy for them both. The summer light faded and lonely shadows gathered in the corners of the room.

'I wish you'd let me go on singing,' Dolly said. 'I'd only just got started when I had to stop.'

'You got married.'

'I could still have gone on singing.'

'Then you had Joe. What about him?'

'Girls manage careers these days as well as husbands and children, so why couldn't they then?'

'Because everything was different. Men liked looking after their wives in those days.'

'You married beneath you,' Dolly said. 'That's why you kept me in the background.'

'Baloney,' said Laddy. 'There's no social difference between a commercial traveller and a gents' outfitter, is there?'

'No, but you were Laddy Silver, weren't you?'

'Laddy Silver.' Raising his hands he stroked with sudden bitterness at the little wisps of hair still struggling to maintain a foothold on his cranium. 'Who the hell was Laddy Silver?'

Without replying Dolly got up from her chair and went through to the bedroom. He heard the squeak of the cupboard doors, then she returned with a heavy leather suitcase thickly covered with travel labels. She put it on the floor between them, and puffing slightly, sat down beside it. The locks clicked open and she began to rummage beneath the open lid.

'Don't,' Laddy said.

'That was Laddy Silver,' she said, and laid a photograph on his lap. The man in it had thick black hair that gleamed like a wet roof, a white bow tie poised on an immaculate dress shirt and a cigarette holder held between delicately manicured fingers.

'When I told my mother we were getting married she said what's the catch? What's he marrying you for when he could have a debutante? I said I didn't know, and she said, well, watch your step. A man in his position wouldn't marry a girl like you if he hadn't got some ulterior motive.'

'You were little and thin, with big eyes and a way of putting over a lyric that no other girl ever had except Ella,' Laddy said. Leaning forward he drew out a handful of publicity stills, of old dinner-dance programmes and a photograph of the band waving from the deck of the *Queen Mary*.

'It hurts,' he said, looking through them. 'No use pretending it doesn't.'

'We haven't been through them for years,' Dolly said. 'Not since Joe was in a skiffle group.'

'Little boy Joe,' Laddy said. 'Remember how I used to play him a lullaby?'

'I remember. He was the only person I wasn't jealous of.'

'There was never any need to be jealous. I only ever loved you, and I dressed you in mink to prove it, didn't I? All mink you were, from head to toe.'

'But all those women who wouldn't leave you alone. Society women giving you gold cigarette cases, waiting outside the hotel suite and freezing me with hate when I came out instead of you . . .'

She sat by the suitcase absently rubbing the cramp in her bulbous calves, unaware that he had left the room until the first notes of music crept through the open door. He was hunched on the side of the bed with the tenor sax catching the last gleam of light. He hadn't played for years and the first experimental scale sounded husky and hesitant, then like the moon sliding from behind a bank of cloud the notes sang clear and silver sweet.

Speechlessly she staggered to her feet and stood leaning against the bedroom doorway with her face tilted blindly towards the sound. He played the lullaby for little Joe, breathing the sounds like a sigh before wandering on through the tunes that still carried the elegant dinner-jacket charm of the Savoy, the Dorchester and the old Trocadero.

She sang with him, but only in her mind, and when the final tune was no more than a bitter-sweet echo in the room she opened her eyes like someone awakening from a long sleep.

'That was Gershwin.'

'I know,' he said, laying the sax carefully back in its velvet-lined case. 'I meant it as a kind of tribute.'

111

She went over to him and he opened his arms. Sitting on the bed he only came up to her chest, and she found herself kissing with sudden passion the bony cranium with its poor little wisps of hair.

They fell backwards, sideways, crying because of Gershwin and laughing because it was all so crazy and because they weren't sure whether they still could any more.

'Listen, sweetie,' Laddy said next day. 'I've got news.'

'Uh-huh?'

They were having breakfast in their bathrobes, a thing they hadn't done for years. The voice of the blackbird came in through the open window.

'We're going to Canada to see Joe. We'll phone him tonight. We could fix a cheap flight, and now that we're – we've no commitments –'

'Now that Gershwin's dead,' she said, dry-eyed.

'Now that we're free, what's to stop us? After all, Joe's our baby. Our real baby –'

'Suppose he doesn't want us? Maybe he's tied up with some woman –'

'Aahh –' Busily he buttered his toast. 'You women are always on about other women. So maybe Joe's got a woman – after all, he's thirty-five and human – but what's that got to do with his poor old Momma and Poppa going to pay him a visit, huh?'

The years had fallen away; Joe was in the forefront of their thoughts in the same way that Laddy had unwittingly slipped back into the transatlantic slang of the dance band days. He looked across at Dolly in her white towelling bathrobe and silver pink curls and called her a cutie.

They discussed the idea of going to Canada with steadily increasing enthusiasm, and after more coffee and toast worked out that it would be silly not to ring Joe with the good news straight away. So they rang him, oblivious of the fact that for him it was three o'clock in the morning.

'Joe – hey, Joey – this is Daddy! This is your old Poppa –'

'Christ, England,' said a blurred voice. 'What's wrong?'

'Nothing's wrong,' roared Laddy, 'except that the old gal and I are coming out to see you! We can come any time, so just give the word . . .'

They talked for fifteen minutes, during which time Joe woke up and said he'd be glad to see them only they mustn't expect things to be the same as they were when he went away. He was a grown man now, and things changed, didn't they?

'Of course they do – ' cried Dolly, leaning over Laddy's shoulder and blasting his eardrum. 'Things have changed for us too, and we'd so love to see you, Joe baby – '

When the line clicked they stood looking at one another with happy tears in their eyes, then Laddy shaved and dressed and set off for the travel agents' while Dolly washed the breakfast things and dusted around.

'But I still think it's a risk,' she said when he returned with a collection of coloured brochures. 'We haven't seen Joe since he was twenty-two – '

'And we're going to be there for his birthday on the 5th of September,' Laddy said.

They sat down and began to plan the details.

'We'll be there to see the Indian summer and you'll have to set to and make him a birthday cake. I bet he's never had a bit of decent cake since he left home.'

'What'll I wear? He'll think I'm so old . . .'

'He'll love you,' Laddy said very seriously. 'Just as much as I do.'

If only he'll love me like he did when he was little, she thought. She could see him so clearly, even without closing her eyes.

They booked the flight, checked the state of their bank account and laughed incredulously at their old passport photographs. Then Laddy sat down to write a long letter to Joe, telling him among many, many other things, when to expect them.

The doorbell rang when Dolly was in the bedroom trying on an old evening dress. Through layers of flame-coloured chiffon she heard Laddy answer it, and then the muffled sound of voices. One belonged to a woman, and Dolly's head burst through the gathered neckline in time to hear it say: 'It just seems like fate, somehow.'

Silent in stockinged feet she went through to the lounge, then halted abruptly. Little Miss Whatsit in jeans and tee-shirt was standing close to Laddy and gently brushing his cheek with something held in her cupped hands.

'She says someone found it outside the Maudesley Hospital,' he said helplessly, 'and she wants to give it to us.'

Without speaking, Dolly stood watching while the girl placed the kitten on Laddy's shoulder. She watched the way it stood up, arching its tiny back and mewing shrilly.

'But we can't – ' she heard Laddy say.

'Oh, Mr Silver, you *must*! The only way to get over losing a pet is to have another one in its memory – ' Her bright silly face beamed at him persuasively. 'And if you don't have him, he'll have to be destroyed.'

'Yes, but – '

'I know you're going to love him just like the way you loved the other one,' she said, then with a brief little wave in Dolly's direction, added: 'Don't worry, I'll see myself out.'

The kitten teetered on Laddy's shoulder, continuing to mew. Carefully he detached its claws from his shirt and stood looking at the way it tried to nestle in the hollow of his hands.

'It wouldn't make any difference,' he said at length. 'We'd still go.'

'Of course it makes a difference,' Dolly said. 'You heard her say it'll be destroyed if we don't keep it.'

'We could put it in a boarding place.'

'No, we couldn't. It'd get fleas and things.'

'But what about Joe?'

'We won't be going,' she said.

He looked up from the kitten and met the accusation in her eyes. The old, old accusation that went back to the days of Society women giving him gold cigarette cases and waiting outside the hotel suite.

'Look, it's only a little helpless kitten,' he said. 'And she meant it for both of us.'

'Put it in Gershwin's basket while I warm some milk for it.'

But the kitten had gone trustingly to sleep in his hands, so he sat quietly on the arm of the chair until she returned, looking sleazy and dishevelled in the old evening dress that was far too tight and all the wrong colour.

'Don't hold him like that, he can't breathe.'

'But we don't want another cat!' he cried, suddenly desperate. 'Honest to Christ, we don't want another one!'

She put the milk down on the floor, then removed the kitten from his hands in a brusque, proprietorial fashion.

'That's what we said about Gershwin,' she said. 'Remember?'

Smokey

Mark Ronson

'I hear that you are deserting our little sanctum for the delights of a Scottish island, young Reggie,' boomed the Colonel as he placed a pile of books on the Afghan Campaigns of 1865-85 on the desk lit by a green-shaded lamp.

'Yes, I'm taking my holiday on Inchcait,' replied a slender, pale-faced young man with spectacles. 'I understand it has a very interesting group of menhirs which have been rather neglected by the experts.' For a moment his light blue eyes gleamed behind his thick lenses, then he was the model librarian again.

'I hope you take some notice of the lassies up there,' the Colonel said jovially. 'I've finished with these – made a nice chapter in my regimental history. Thanks for your help in finding them. Don't know how this place would run without you.'

The same evening while Reginald Meredith carefully packed his photographic equipment he told his mother what the Colonel – who was one of the library governors – had said.

'I'm so glad, dear,' she replied. 'The Richardson does seem to suit you. So much better than that awful public library. Being able to take a long holiday in the summer does give you an opportunity to do your field work.'

She smiled brightly at him over her sewing, but mentally she echoed the Colonel's sentiment about the lassies. Her son was now in his early thirties and, apart from that disastrous engagement to Marion a decade ago, he had taken very little interest in young ladies. Ever since his father's death so long ago, Reginald had been quiet and studious, and she liked to believe that the reason he had not married was because he had not found Miss Right yet. Her one objection to the Richardson – a private reference library founded a century ago for respectable authors and upper class literati – was that he was unlikely to find Miss Right there.

'I want you to take extra socks and make sure you have your watertight boots,' Mrs Meredith said. 'I'm sure you'll be tramping over mires and goodness knows what, and I don't want you ill with a cold as you were after your trip to the Merry Maidens. I sometimes wonder if all this work in nasty bleak places will be worth it.'

'It will be someday,' Reginald said with conviction. 'Inchcait is pretty remote and it may take a letter a while to reach you, so you mustn't worry if you don't hear from me for a bit.'

'I'll be all right with Mrs Foch for company.' His mother looked fondly at the beautiful white Persian cat curled up on the sofa.

Reginald reached over and combed his fingers through the silky fur of the animal who opened her pink mouth and yawned elegantly. Since childhood he had loved cats. They possessed qualities which he would have liked to possess – independence which bordered on arrogance, grace of movement and lithe sexuality.

There was mystery in Mrs Foch's green eyes which particularly appealed to him. Mysteries were his passion.

Reginald stood in the bows of the fishing boat which doubled as the Inchcait ferry, watching the scattering of houses behind the island's jetty materialize out of the morning mist. To his relief the sea between Oban and his destination had been as smooth as oil, and he had enjoyed gliding through the white vapour which shrouded it. If it had not been for the muffled thump of the boat's Diesel there would have been nothing to remind him of the twentieth century.

He almost felt he could be journeying through some supernatural realm. He remembered research he had done on Scottish legends about mortals who had entered the fairy world. Usually the results had been tragic because fairies had a different time scale to humans.

As the boat drew inshore a wind sighed in from the Atlantic, shredding the mist to reveal the island which was to be his home for the next three weeks. It was low lying apart from a hump of a hill in the centre and, while it was not exactly inhospitable, there was a desolate air about it. This, Reginald suddenly realized, was caused by the absence of trees. In the south he had been accustomed to wooded landscapes.

No, it was not only the lack of trees – there was something else, but what it was he could not say. Inchcait certainly had its own atmosphere, just as Iona to the north had a mystic aura which had made it important to pagans and Christians alike.

Water churned to froth beneath the stern of the vessel as the blue-jerseyed skipper manoeuvred it with contemptuous skill alongside the jetty on which a small group of islanders watched in silence. No doubt eager for mail and provisions from the mainland, they made fast the lines which the crew tossed them.

With a clatter which sent the gulls screaming, the winch broke into fuming life and began to hoist a crate out of the hold. Reginald picked up his suitcase and holdall and, after thanking the taciturn skipper, stepped on to the jetty.

He noticed that most of the bystanders were elderly and he guessed that the young people must have been lured away to the cities. It was understandable, the life of a crofter in such a spot must be very hard. And yet as the sun broke through the clouds Inchcait did have a picturesque quality which owed much to the heather tints on the central hill.

'Could you please direct me to Mrs Campbell's house,' Reginald asked an old man who was regarding him with shameless curiosity.

'Ay, it's the widow you are wanting right enough,' he answered. Reginald was delighted with the accent, so much softer than he had expected.

'You'll be the laddie come to board with her,' said another old fellow. 'We dinna get many tourists on Inchcait.'

Reginald realized he would have to give some answers before he received any. The islanders had formed a half-circle round him. Their weatherbeaten faces were impassive, but he sensed they were waiting for him to talk so that he would provide the current fireside topic.

'Actually,' he began, not wishing to go into details about his work, 'I'm a photographer.'

'With a camera?' said the first old man. 'You'll be taking pictures of the seals?'

'It's pretty out at Seal Point,' said a stout woman in an ex-army greatcoat. She chuckled for no apparent reason. 'There's plenty of seabirds over on the other side . . . and wild cats.'

117

The others looked away as though disapproving of some unexplained levity, but she continued unabashed. 'You'll be wanting the way. Go past those cottages and head inland along the track which runs past Sluagh Hill. You should reach Mrs Campbell's in half an hour. Will you be staying long with her?'

'Thank you,' said Reginald. 'Thank you.'

The stares of the islanders made him feel uneasy, and it was with a small sense of relief that he made his way towards the white-washed cottages. Here he was subjected to silent scrutiny by women pegging out their washing. There was something a little odd about these folk. He had noticed they hardly spoke to the crew of the ferry and the sailors had remained equally curt.

Within a couple of minutes the cottages fell behind him, and he was tempted to whistle as he strode along the track. Water in the ruts made by Inchcait's only tractor shone with the reflected blue of the sky. Bracken grew on either side and Reginald observed with pleasure the bejewelled webs decorating it. He was tempted to stop, unpack his camera and try for some close-ups. His new starburst filter would enhance the diamante effect. But he forgot about it the moment he looked up and saw the girl.

Her fine-boned beauty made Reginald catch his breath. Above her homespun skirt she wore a crimson sweater which made a striking contrast with her pale skin and glossy black hair which, when the wind seized it, made him think of black flames. She was the sort of girl he had dreamed about in secret moments, and it was the ideal she represented which had kept him single. He would never settle for second best, for a suitable sensible girl who lacked the fire to stir his imagination and his loins. He had always been fascinated by the woman who was free, unpredictable, intelligent and beautiful. And he knew how unlikely the chances were of such a creature falling in love with a shy librarian.

'A happy return to Inchcait,' she called in the soft voice of the island. 'I'm Meg Campbell, and you have to be Mr Meredith. I came to guide you but the ferry must have been a bit ahead of schedule for once.'

As she came closer Reginald grew aware of her greenish eyes — eyes which reminded him of Mrs Foch.

'You must be confusing me with someone else,' he told her as she led the way along the path carrying his holdall. 'I have never been to Inchcait before.'

'Oh, that is the traditional island greeting to a stranger,' she said. 'It's one of those funny old folk customs. I think it must go back to the Druids who believed in reincarnation. It was once the belief here that if you were born on Inchcait you would return in a later life. So we still say "happy return" to a stranger in case it's someone coming home.'

'What a charming idea,' said Reginald and Meg gave him an amused glance at his choice of words.

On the other side of Sluagh Hill Reginald found that the ground sloped gently westwards towards a sea of Mediterranean blue.

'It's not always grey seas and fog,' the girl said when she noticed his surprise. 'But come, Mother will have the kettle singing.'

Inside the massive walls of the farmhouse where Meg lived with her mother it was as clean and bright as a Christmas card illustration. Reginald found Mrs Campbell to be so placid and comfortable it was hard to imagine that she had given birth to such an exciting daughter.

'It's the wildlife you'll be interested in,' she said when they sat in the cosy kitchen after Reginald had approved his room under the eaves.

'Actually, no,' he said, balancing a blue and white china cup of steaming tea. 'The truth is that I am working on a book about ancient standing stones and the mythology which has grown up around them. I've come here to take pictures of the Grey Cats.'

'You'll get damp feet if you're not careful,' laughed Mrs Campbell. 'It's terrible boggy round the Cats. Meg had better go with you at first.'

'Do you know any legends about the Cat stones?'

Mrs Campbell laughed at the idea. 'They're just a ring of old Druid stones,' she said.

Reginald curbed his desire to explain that they had probably stood for a thousand years before Druidism came to Britain, and merely commented that it was an odd name to give them.

'From some angles – and if you really stretch your imagination – the stones do look like a circle of sitting cats,' said Meg. 'When you're ready I'll take you there and you can see for yourself.

'Fantastic!' Reginald exclaimed. 'They're fantastic.'

119

The vivid blue sea made a dramatic backdrop for the megaliths. Bright sunshine illuminated them perfectly, bringing out their wood-like graining which was the result of centuries of weathering.

Meg sat on one and watched while Reginald unpacked his equipment.

'You must have done some research on the stones – didn't you come across any legends about them?' she asked.

'Yes,' he said as he pulled out the legs of his tripod. 'I read the usual one about them being petrified creatures. This was a very common explanation in olden days. In Cumbria Long Meg and Her Daughters were said to have been witches who were petrified by the wizard Michael Scott, and in Oxfordshire a witch turned an army into the Rollright Stones.

'In the library where I work in London I did come across a book on folklore, published a couple of centuries ago in Edinburgh, in which a tradition was mentioned that the people of Inchcait once had the power to change themselves into cats.'

'So the poor things were punished by being turned into stone,' said Meg with a laugh.

'Once you start going into these legends you find that they get pretty mixed up,' Reginald said. 'The truth behind the werecat story was probably that, being an out-lying spot, a pagan festival continued into medieval times with people dressing up in animal skins. It was not unusual, and you still get a hint of it with the Abbots Bromley Horn Dancers.

'Then, as time passed, the vague memory of this was worked into a story connected with the stones whose shapes suggested the idea of cats.'

'You make it sound rather dull. Perhaps we could revive the pagan festival and start a tourist boom.'

For a moment he took her seriously, then she burst into laughter.

Ignoring the damp, Reginald knelt on the turf and moved his old Rolleiflex until the viewfinder was filled with a superb composition of the Grey Cats. His spectacles flashed his enthusiasm. He knew that he must take advantage of the bright light as there might not be such a sunny day for the rest of his stay.

Meg left him, explaining that she had to see to her mother's sheep which were grazing on the slopes of Sluagh Hill. He was loading another roll of Ektachrome in the shade of a megalith when he glanced up and saw a large grey cat looking at him from the top of the next stone.

For a moment Reginald wondered whether he was a wild cat. He certainly looked as though he could survive as an outdoor hunter with his deep chest and powerful limbs. A scarred ear and a dangerous gleam in his yellow eyes suggested that he was not averse to fighting. Then the photographer was struck by the cat's appropriate choice of a vantage point. If he could get a picture of the animal perched there it would make a pleasing illustration and add a touch of light relief to *The Mythology of British Prehistoric Monuments* by R.T. Meredith.

'Good boy, Smokey,' he said soothingly while he wound on the film. 'Stay put, Smokey, old fellow.'

The cat watched him coldly while he focussed the camera, but before Reginald could press the shutter release he appeared to leap out of the viewfinder. When Reginald searched for him among the stones it seemed that Smokey had lived up to his impromptu name.

After a generous supper Reginald left Meg and Mrs Campbell listening to their battery radio, and climbed the stairs to his bedroom with its sloping ceiling and hint of camphor. The sea air and unaccustomed exercise ensured that he was asleep almost as soon as he got into the old bed with its real feather mattress.

Then the dream began.

Reginald was moving through an enchanted world of black shadow and silver light. He was strangely excited by the near full moon riding serenely among tatters of fleeing cloud. He was aware that he was heading for the stone circle he had been photographing that day, and his pulse raced with the feeling that he was on the edge of a marvellous threshold. Anything could happen on a night such as this, and afterwards life would never be quite the same.

Ahead the ground rose like a petrified ocean wave, and suddenly on its crest he saw a figure silhouetted against the moon's disc – a figure that he had no difficulty in recognizing.

'Meg!' he called. She turned her head, and the night wind streamed her hair and plucked at her dark cloak-like garment. Then she was over the brow.

Reginald ran after her, and never in his life had he been able to move so easily and fast. Soon he made out the stone circle, crouching shapes defined by the luminous sea in the background. He passed two of the largest megaliths and found Meg standing in the centre of the ring.

Like everything on this bewitching night, she was different as he was different. Her features were more clear cut, her body more supple and her eyes turned the moonlight into jade.

'A happy return to Inchcait,' she said as she approached him, bright lips smiling and her arms ready to embrace.

'Meg,' he murmured and she was in his arms. They kissed with such passion that he could feel the impression of her sharp teeth through her lips.

'Do you want me to be yours?' she asked.

'Of course.'

'As you did before?'

He did not know what to say, her question puzzled him.

She stepped back and unfastened the clasp of her cloak. It rustled to the turf and she was ivory nude and the wind blowing her hair made him think of dark flames again – and there was a dark flame within him which dried his throat and quickened the drumbeat of his pulse. He almost stumbled as he reached for her, and at that moment a cloud extinguished the moon.

And, in the way of dreams, when the cloud slid away and the cold light returned to the megaliths, Reginald found that the world had changed. The stones had grown to an enormous size, and beyond them the earth was vast. He had changed too. He knew he had lost his clothes yet he did not feel the chill of the night wind. He was aware of scents and vibrations which he had never known before, all telling him secrets he had not the words to describe.

He looked for Meg and saw that – like him – she had changed into a cat.

As Reginald squelched towards the Grey Cats he half expected them to have gained some special significance – perhaps to appear larger as they had in his dream. But when he saw them in the morning light they appeared to be a commonplace aspect of the landscape. Today the sky was overcast and the sea behind the megaliths leaden, creating an atmosphere which was reflected by his mood. Reginald was physically and mentally exhausted, and as he began to take measurements with a surveyor's tape, he found it difficult to concentrate on the work.

After he had woken up the previous night, filled with relief to find himself beneath the patchwork quilt, he had tried to convince himself that the extraordinary dream had been the result of overwork. He had put in a lot of unpaid overtime to get a microfilm system established before he went on holiday. It was obvious that his fatigued mind had reacted to the new impressions it had received on Inchcait – the beautiful girl, the stone circle and the talk of cats. The result had been a vivid fantasy.

Yet as he tramped from stone to stone, he wondered if that was all there was to it. The dream had seemed so real that he could not get it out of his mind, and he found an almost erotic pleasure in remembering what it had been like to be covered with fur . . .

At mid-morning a wall of clammy mist rolled in from the sea so that the further stones became indistinct shadows. And he heard Meg's voice before he could see her.

'Morning, Mr Meredith,' she called. 'I thought a thermos of coffee might be welcome.'

'How kind of you.'

'Mother thought you looked rather pale this morning,' she said as she walked into vision.

'I had a bad night. A strange dream. I think this sometimes happens when you find yourself in a different environment. The mind has to cope with so much that is new to it.'

'I believe some people do have vivid dreams when they come to Inchcait,' she said as she unscrewed the cap of the flask. 'Was it interesting, Mr Meredith?'

Her greeny eyes were upon him. For a mad moment he felt that she knew exactly what he had dreamed, and he blushed – and then thought how ridiculous he was being.

When he took the drink from her, her hand rested on his wrist and for a long moment they looked into each other's faces. And in that moment Reginald realized that he was deeply in love with this girl. That could be an explanation of the dream. No doubt a psychiatrist would have been delighted with such a textbook example of the unconscious mind endeavouring to influence the conscious.

Meg broke the spell by turning to the large sheet of graph paper on which he had been mapping the position of the stones. As he began to explain it to her, a slight movement caught his eye. The cat Smokey was watching them from one of the mist-veiled megaliths.

That evening Reginald thoroughly enjoyed his supper with Meg and her mother. Nothing but common-place remarks were passed, and yet he was certain he was not imagining the attraction which was developing between himself and this exciting island girl.

When he said goodnight to Mrs Campbell, Meg walked with him to the foot of the stairs and gave him a quick kiss before vanishing into her own room. As Reginald undressed he smiled at what she might think if she ever learned what he had dreamed about her. It was one secret which he must keep.

Next morning he woke in time to have breakfast with Meg and then set out happily to the Grey Cats. The light was clear today and he decided to take some photographs of individual stones before returning to his measuring. He was particularly interested in the graining of the stone, and he hoped to get some intriguing effects as he set up his tripod.

'You're a photographer, I'm thinking,' said a voice behind him. He straightened and saw a burly young man in wellingtons and a duffel coat.

'As you can see I do take photographs,' Reginald said. There was something about the stranger which made him wary.

'I'm wondering if I could hire you to take some snaps for me.'

'Well . . .' began Reginald not sure what to think.

'You see,' the man continued, his weatherbeaten face without expression, 'I'm getting wed soon and I want a snap of it. I'm getting wed to Meg Campbell. It's been agreed since we were small. You understand?'

The blood drained from Reginald's face. For a moment he felt dizzy.

'So you can take the snaps. I think I'd like that.'

'But I'm only here for a short while,' Reginald heard himself explain.

'Then we must bring the ceremony forward. Bring it forward we must so that you can snap us. It's time Meg were a wife. She's a restless one at the moment, and this sometimes gives the wrong idea. I mean, the wrong idea to people who don't know her well. People like strangers. And that could lead to trouble.'

He leaned forward as though to tell Reginald something in confidence.

'What I mean by trouble is that I'd slaughter anyone who came between Meg and me with no more remorse than I feel when I slaughter a sheep.'

He walked away, pausing once to shout over his shoulder, 'Don't forget, I want you to take the snaps.'

At supper Reginald said to Meg, 'I met a friend of yours at the Grey Cats this morning.'

'Oh yes,' she said, and he noticed that Mrs Campbell gave her daughter an uneasy glance.

'Yes. I don't know his name, but he asked me to take your wedding photographs.'

'Andrew!' exclaimed Meg. 'You must take no heed of Andrew. He's mad.'

'I rather gathered from him that the two of you were sort of . . . engaged.'

'Meg and he used to walk out when they were both little more than children,' said Mrs Campbell. 'It was harmless and it did not last for long, but he still believes this gives him some right to Meg. On Inchcait they think it would be a good match, but Meg has too much spirit for the likes of him.'

'And do you think it would be a good match?'

'Och, it could be worse. Andrew McLeod's a strange man, but he's a bonnie crofter, and I think it best that island folk wed island folk. There are some things which strangers would find difficult to understand about us.'

That night Reginald dreamed again he was a cat. It was as though the dream was permanent – a mirror existence – to which he returned to be intoxicated by the moonlight in the circle and the lithe form of Meg. Her eyes glowed close to his, and her dark fur gave him tiny electric shocks when it rubbed against his. Sometimes she nipped him playfully, and sometimes she put her paw on his neck and licked him. Both knew the time for mating was near. His heart was filled with a mysterious joy which humans lost when they distanced themselves from nature – when they ceased to venerate Pan and became anxious about their souls. It captivated him so fully that he was startled to hear a long wail of ecstasy, then realized it had come from his own throat.

Suddenly flirtatious, Meg sprang on to the top of a megalith. He was about to follow when something struck him so hard that he was flung to the ground. There was a snarling in his ear and a feline face close to his, teeth bright in the moonlight and hate blazing from yellow eyes.

Over and over the two cats rolled. Smokey's teeth fastened on the fur of Reginald's neck, but he managed to wrench himself away and crouch with his chest close to the grass.

For a split second he looked at the stone rearing above him on which Meg sat with her tail demurely over her forepaws. He had hoped for some sign of encouragement but she remained as enigmatic as the stone beneath her.

Smokey rushed to the attack. As Reginald threw himself back upon his haunches, the grey cat's claws sliced his face. The pain and the fear, coupled with the knowledge that he was no match for the warrior cat, made Reginald flee from the circle. He woke up in the room with the sloping ceiling.

The horror of the nightmare was heavy upon him. He felt ill, and lit his bedside candle. Then he got up and went to the water jug on the chest-of-drawers.

He wondered if he was going insane. Would he dream the next night and find himself back in the circle to continue the terrible combat?

He gulped a glass of water, and saw his face in the mirror. He almost screamed, not with pain but at the implication of the blood trickling down his cheek.

The women hanging out their washing gazed at Reginald silently as he carried his suitcase and holdall past their cottages.

Meg had been missing from breakfast when he told Mrs Campbell that he intended to leave on the morning's ferry. She had murmured politely that she was sure he knew best, but her eyes remained fixed on his furrowed cheek.

When he reached the jetty there were the same old men lounging on it, watching him through their pipe smoke with impassive eyes as he dropped his bags on the planking.

'Has the ferry gone?' he gasped, pressing the stitch in his side.

'It's not gone,' one said finally. Then to dash Reginald's relief he added, 'It aint' gone because it ain't been. Broken down in Oban harbour. Maybe a week before the engine's repaired. Looks like you're marooned, mister.'

There was a chuckle from the others.

As Reginald began the return journey across Inchcait he realized it was inevitable that he should stay on the island. There was no avoiding fate, and the knowledge that he was about to come face to face with it brought a strange sense of relief.

Meg was waiting by the farmhouse door. The life seemed to have gone out of her as she murmured she was sorry that he had not been able to leave as he had wished.

'Of course you can stay here until the boat comes,' she said. 'And there's no need to go to the Grey Cats any more.'

'I believe it's full moon tonight,' said Reginald. 'I am going to photograph the stones in the moonlight. It should provide a very dramatic effect.' He paused while she looked at him with sudden understanding.

'It'll be quite exciting,' he added, 'to be there in the flesh, in the circle . . . alone with Smokey.'

The Great God Mau

Stella Whitelaw

In the calendar-less days before man, violent changes within active volcanoes threw rock into new mountain ranges and created immense ravines flooded with water. At the same time a new species of animal appeared. It was a small, short legged animal with a sleek body and a long tail. It was called Miacis. It was destined to found a family of mammals – the dog, the weasel, the raccoon, civet, hyenas and the cat.

When Man emerged, he hunted for food but he did not eat cats. He found them too useful merely to eat. He discovered that they could protect his precious stores of grain by keeping down the rats and mice. So the cat became the protector of granaries and in Ancient Egypt was as sacred as the Gods themselves.

The cat goddess was called Bast, or Bastet. She was also known as Pasht. She was portrayed as a tall, slim woman with a cat's head, holding a musical instrument, a shield and a basket of kittens. Her temple was built at Bubastis, east of the Nile delta and was more beautiful than any other temple.

The cat of Ancient Egypt was an elegant, strikingly marked spotted tabby, long of neck and shoulder, reddish brown in colour and altogether a handsome creature with great poise and presence. Cats were also kept to guard the family from poisonous snakes, and there were strict laws to protect them. To kill a cat meant the death penalty.

Mau was one such valued cat of Ancient Egypt. He was regularly taken to the vast temple of the cat goddess at Bubastis. The long journey was made in a gold boat from Thebes to the temple and Mau was accompanied by his own servants. The Pharaoh travelled in another boat and so did his Queen. They arrived with pomp and ceremony for feasts held in honour of Bastet.

Mau was always a little in awe of the splendour of the temple, but he did not show it. Towering red granite blocks dominated the great square, with canals on either side one hundred feet wide and in the centre was the shrine to the goddess surrounded by tall date palms. The walls of the temple were richly decorated in every colour with scenes of kings presenting gifts to the goddess. She was as important as the great god Ra.

Almost the same reverence was bestowed upon Mau. He was allowed to roam the deck of his boat, returning to his silken pillow to sleep. He wore a gold ear-ring in his large, pointed ear and he had a jewelled collar studded with emeralds to match his fathomless eyes. On special days he also wore a bronze chain and sacred pendant hung about his neck, and an amulet of the sacred eye which represented the solar eye of the god Horus. Mau tolerated the jewels, though he was always glad when they were removed and put away in a golden chest.

There was also a cat cemetery at Bubastis and many Egyptian families would bring the embalmed bodies of their pet cats for ritual burial. The small bodies were wrapped in linen or in simple cases made of straw. Some came in a casket or cat-shaped box.

Mau knew nothing of these burials. He was venerated by the Pharaoh and his Queen, and lived a life of luxury in return for the remarkable power which the great god Bastet could evoke against sickness and evil. But Mau was not worshipped as Bastet was worshipped, although to the Pharaoh, the cat was sacred and no one cared to dispute the fact.

Mau's sacred role began in this way. One day the Pharaoh and his Queen were hunting in the Nile marshes when suddenly the cat appeared among the reeds with three waterfowl. He had one bird gripped in his jaws and the two others held tightly in his claws.

The royal party were overcome by the sudden presence of Mau. It seemed to them that the cat was a re-incarnation of the cat depicted on the tomb painting of Pharaoh Thutmoses II and his Queen Hatshepsut, who had been gathering lotus blossoms in their light papyrus boat when a similarly remarkable cat had appeared to them.

It was taken as a special sign and Mau returned with them to the Pharaoh's palace and was proclaimed sacred. Not being born to such nobility, Mau insisted on a certain degree of freedom. The palace covered a large area and Mau spent his days inspecting the great halls and vast granaries. He knew every inch of the spacious courtyards, gardens and rooms, as if he had been the architect himself.

Each morning he went to the pool with its shady trees, where he could sharpen his claws and frighten the silly ducks. He watched the servants drawing water from the wells, then skirted the cattle yards and dog kennels. He did not care for the smells from these places.

His favourite part of the palace were the stewards' rooms next to the kitchens and food stores, for although Mau was fed with chicken and fish from a golden bowl at the Pharaoh's table, a little snack never came amiss. Here the servants gave him delicious nibbles and goats milk.

The Pharaoh never knew of these early morning visits and would often remark: 'How fastidious Mau is with his food. See how he picks only the best from the fish. How little he eats. A true god is fed from the spirit within.'

In fact the true god was rarely hungry for he also visited the Queen's suite and her womens' rooms where they teased him with sweetmeats and brushed his fur with silver brushes. They painted his nails with a shining coloured enamel, and Mau thought this peculiar and rather pointless.

At mid-day Mau strolled through the great audience hall to the Window of Appearances where the Pharaoh held his daily public court and gave gifts and rewards. Mau always appeared with him. He sat in the portico, long and elegant, quietly unmoved by the cheering crowds. The people thought it an excellent sign that he should be there. It meant that Bastet was regarding them with favour.

A servant was sweeping the floor between the two rows of columns in preparation for a great feast that was to be held. Mau liked the servant; his name was Thut. He was a simple but strong young man and he was kind to Mau, sometimes forgetting that he was a god and treating him as an ordinary cat. Mau appreciated this and he also liked Merya, the girl that Thut was always talking to in the kitchens. She had beautiful hair that rippled like silk.

Mau watched the broom of rushes sweeping rhythmically across

130

the floor. He crouched down, his long black-tipped tail whipping from side to side. He would dearly love to pounce on that broom and send it skidding across the marble tiles. Thut realised that Mau was watching and gave the broom a few quick jerks to tease the cat.

Mau's whiskers twitched. He would not be able to resist it much longer. A small growl grew in his throat. The Pharaoh heard the sound and felt that Bastet must be displeased. He immediately doubled the gold he was about to give to an old steward who was leaving after many years in his service. The old man fell on his arthritic knees and mumbled his astonished thanks.

At night Mau was put to sleep on a gold silk pillow in a special shrine in the chapel. The pillow was slippery and uncomfortable, so he often toured the granaries at night, roaming the vast storehouses and inspecting the corn bins. Then towards dawn he would go to the servants' quarters. He knew the room that Merya shared with the other women and he would curl up at her feet, careful not to wake her.

'Oh Mau,' she whispered one night in a terrified voice. 'Something terrible will happen to me if I am caught sleeping with a god.'

When there were ceremonies in the Sanctuary, Mau awoke to the sound of the priest chanting hymns. He allowed them to bath him in perfume and put a wide collar of linked gold round his neck. Then Mau was carried in his boat shrine by a procession of priests to the outer court of the Great Temple. Granite statues of the Pharaoh towered above him, each toe the size of a table, and the great columns rose to the roof and into sunburst paintings of reeds and the papyrus flower and lotus buds. It was very spectacular and the endless singing was enough to send him to sleep. If he began to doze, the priests whispered among themselves, so Mau kept himself awake with day dreams of catching the painted birds that decorated the columns.

'We will go down the Nile to the Valley of Kings,' said the Pharaoh. 'I want to see how my work is progressing.'

Mau was quite happy to go anywhere. They disembarked at one of the landing stages and were led along a causeway to the foot of the cliffs. A large number of ramps were in place, and stones were being dragged on sledges up the slopes by lines of workers roped together. There were thousands of workers drawn from the peasants who could not work in the fields when the Nile was flooded. Long conveys of barges had brought the stones from distant quarries and oxen had dragged them from the banks. The skilled masons were shaping and preparing the rocks and the noise was deafening.

Mau thought it all very dusty and noisy. He sneezed twice. So many people milling about . . . he was glad that Thut was among the servants carrying his gold food bowls. He watched the water being poured in front of the sledges to help them slide up the ramps, and tried to close his ears to the man beating time with clappers so that the strength of the workmen could be united. The men groaned and gasped under the hot Egyptian sun as they strained to drag the huge blocks of stone up the ramps into position.

Mau could not see the point of all this frantic activity when they could fish in the Nile or merely sit in the sun and doze. He made a pretence of lordly supervision for about ten minutes, but then boredom took over and he retreated to the shade of his boat shrine and went to sleep.

'See, the great god Mau is content,' said the Pharaoh with satisfaction. 'He is pleased with the work. He is meditating with the gods and leaves this great work in my hands.'

The workers cheered, believing him, though the Pharaoh had not touched one trowelful of soil. And the work went on.

One night some time later Mau was prowling among the granaries when he became aware of people hurrying. The fur on his back stood up – the atmosphere had changed. It was charged with something he did not understand. For a moment, he was alarmed, every sense alert.

'But where is the great god Mau?' they whispered among themselves. 'Where is Mau? We must find Mau.'

'Here he is,' said Merya, with tears in her voice.

A procession of boats left Thebes and went down the Nile. Mau lost count of the number of boats. He had never seen such a procession, each boat laden with rare carvings and statues, jars of wine and oil, pitchers of milk, chests of gold and jewels, papyrus scrolls and valuable ornaments. There were platters of fruit and bread, even live birds caught by the legs with twine.

132

Perhaps they were going to have a special feast, thought Mau, as they reached the landing stage. It certainly looked like it. He watched with interest as the birds fluttered helplessly. He was not hungry, but he always enjoyed a quick pounce.

A long line of priests and servants formed by the landing stage. They began dragging a boat-shaped sledge covered with lotus flowers. The Queen followed, wailing and weeping, throwing dust on her head.

The procession went first to the Mortuary Temple where rituals were carried out and jars filled with organs. Mau could not understand why no one would look at him, not even Thut. The priests then carried out the ceremony of Opening of the Mouth in front of the chapel and the sacred tablets were put on the eyes and mouth of the dead Pharaoh by his eldest son. Mau felt a cold shiver along his spine even though the sun was hot as the mummy was lowered down the shaft.

Mau found himself being carried through a narrow entrance into the rock and then along a dark passage. He did not like it, but could see from the flickering torches that the walls were carved with inscriptions and scenes from the Pharaoh's life – hunting and fishing and feasting. They passed storehouses filled with furniture and household goods. The procession went deeper and deeper into the heart of the rock and Mau could smell the dampness even though wells had been dug to drain away flood water.

They came at last to a small chamber where the mummy was placed in a great stone sarcophagus. The walls were covered with paintings and the scent of musk and spices was strong.

'I think it's cruel,' muttered Thut. 'The practice of burying the king's household was abandoned years ago, thank goodness,' he added, thinking of his own skin and Merya's.

'The great god Mau will ensure the safe passage of our dead king through the underworld,' said a priest. 'He will help him answer the questions of the forty-two animal and human-headed gods. Then the god Osiris will see that Mau is returned to us. You will see.'

Thut hoped he was right. He was very fond of Mau, god or no god. The cat had given him comfort and, in a strange way, a hope for the future.

Mau was sitting alert on his golden cushion, his pointed ears pricked for any new sound that would solve the mystery of the day's events. He was wearing the heaviest of his ceremonial collars and that was a bad sign. The collar rubbed on his shoulder bones and he hoped Thut would take it off soon.

They all heard a low rumble and then the chamber resounded with thuds as the work began of filling in the shaft with rocks and earth. The priests hurried through their last ceremonies although they were in no danger.

Thut put his hand briefly on Mau's head and touched the short reddish fur. 'Farewell, old friend,' he whispered.

The movement caught the attention of a priest. 'You dare to touch the great god Mau,' he hissed. 'You will be punished.'

'Only for luck, for luck,' the young Thut pleaded, bowing his head. 'I am humble before the god. I am his servant.'

'Out of the way,' the priests swept past and retraced their steps through the passageways and staircases to the main entrance of the tomb. They gave the command for the entrance to be sealed and hidden.

Mau did not pay much attention to his surroundings at first. He thought it a pretty odd game and waited for someone to come and fetch him. He knew where a mouse was hiding in the granaries and was keen to chase him out.

He sneezed as the dust settled around him, and the noise stopped echoing in the chamber. He had the feeling he was alone. He stretched his legs and jumped off the cushion. It was then he discovered that his collar was fastened with a length of chain to the ornamental carved stool on which lay his cushion. He growled at the chain and shook it angrily. He tugged and leaped this way and that but he was jerked back by the linked gold plates hard against his neck.

He crouched at the full length of the chain, his tail flicking with fury. But he was feeling his first tremors of fear. He had never been chained before. Again he attacked the chain, the stool, the cushion. He lay exhausted and slept.

When he awoke he thought he was back at the palace, near the gardens and shady tree-lined pool. Then he remembered from the darkness, the smell and the heavy collar that he was still a prisoner. He twisted and turned in the collar, flattening his ears and trying to drag it over his skull. He began to scratch at the carved stool but it was a hard wood, and it seemed hours before his claws made even a small groove.

He cried out, a loud strident call that echoed down the passageways. The candles fluttered in deep pools of wax and the incense drifted away to the ceiling of the tomb. It was getting very cold.

As time passed Mau was racked with hunger and thirst. He knew he was getting weaker. He knew he must find food before he lost the strength to move. With a tremendous effort he dragged the stool across the rock floor, the collar biting into his neck and almost choking him. Many times he had to stop and rest. Then he knocked into one of the pitchers and it fell over, water flowing onto the floor and gathering in little pools. Mau drank eagerly, his parched tongue lapping in weak gulps like a kitten.

He found wide necked earthenware jars of corn and dates. His primeval ancestor, the Miacis, had eaten fruit. Mau chewed, not caring what he ate. Perhaps if he was very quick, he would catch a lizard. His neck was a mass of open sores from dragging the stool around. He grew thinner and the collar began to get loose, but still he could not pull his head free. The craftsman who had made the heavy gold ornament had measured him carefully.

Days and weeks went by. Mau was living in hell. He was constantly in pain from the festering sores. The corn and dates had long since gone and now he ate the candle wax from the dark pools. He had almost forgotten the outside world, but he clung to life. His dreams were confused, and his thin limbs twitched with memories.

He hardly heard the soft footsteps of the robbers as they crept stealthily and warily down the passageway. Their burning torches cast long shadows on the walls and it was this light that Mau first noticed through half-closed eyes. He kept quite still as the figures crept into the burial chamber. Mau trusted no one.

The men were dark-faced and in ragged robes. They were whispering and trembling with nerves. They touched the stone sarcophagus with awe at first, but they had levers in their hands and were soon seeking a crack. Mau lay in the shadows, watching them, his fluttering heart beating weakly against his ribs.

A flame spluttered and threw a brief streak of light onto Mau's collar. One of the robbers saw the gleam of gold. His eyes glinted.

135

'Gold,' he whispered excitedly. 'Look at this! It's solid gold.' He peered at the corpse of a dead cat lying in the gloom. His gnarled fingers fumbled at the heavy clasp of the collar and found the way to unfasten it. It snapped open. Mau gathered his remaining strength to emit a piercing howl.

'M . . . A . . . U . . . ' He yeowelled with ear-splitting clarity.

The robbers shrieked with fear, dropped their levers and fell over each other in their haste to leave the chamber. They ran, moaning with fear, their hands over their ears as Mau's cries rang through the passageways.

'Mau . . . the great god Mau,' they whimpered as they stumbled through the darkness. Mau flew after them, brushing through their legs in the dark, and the touch of his fur sent them into further paroxisms of terror. 'Ah . . . the god . . . the god. Save us, be merciful and save us,' they cried.

They clambered and slithered over the rocks that they had dug through at the entrance, their hands slippery with sweat. Mau smelled the fresh air and leaped in front of them, sensing freedom at last. He streaked towards the glimmer of light, unseen in the grey shadows, a great surge of willpower giving him strength.

He tumbled out of the narrow hole into the desert night. He paused momentarily, amazed at the brightness of the desert stars in the velvet black sky and the heady oxygen of the cool night air. Then he fled like the wind, not caring in which direction he ran, rejoicing in the feel of the balmy air that stirred through the wisps of fur on his sore skin and the sheer joy of being free . . .

The new Pharaoh had brought his own servants and all the former servants were sent to do other work. Thut had become a brickmaker and he worked hard making bricks from the mud of the fields after the annual floods. Merya spun cloth and brewed beer for the workers and they lived together in a small terraced house that had only a matting of reeds for a roof.

Thut was laying bricks in the sun to dry when Mau approached him. The cat had been walking for many days and his fur was matted with dust. At first Thut was frightened, like the robbers, but when Mau twisted himself round Thut's bare ankles, demanding attention, Thut realized that this was no spirit but Mau alive. He wrapped the cat in a piece of linen and took him to Merya.

'Look at his poor sores,' she said, tears in her eyes. 'And he's so thin. Bastet has sent him to us to be cared for.'

She fed him goats' milk and fish that Thut had caught in the river, and put a soothing ointment on the sores. Mau did not move as she administered the herbal balm. The matted hut was no palace but it seemed he still had his servants.

That night he curled up at Merya's feet, a deep purr of contentment throbbing and swelling in his throat. He would sleep now, with complete trust in the two humans.

'But if they know that we have the great god Mau, we will be punished,' Thut whispered to his wife, too distracted to sleep.

'Ssh . . . ' said Merya, stroking his thick dark hair as if he were a child. 'Who will know? One cat is very much like another. And who would expect to see Mau here? Of all places?'

She got up very early the next morning before it was light and took a file from her small box of precious possessions. Mau again sat quite still as she patiently filed away at his claws. It was ticklish and occasionally he twitched at the light sensation, longing to lick between his toes and be done with the pedicure.

Carefully Merya gathered every fragment of gold off his claws and put it away in a small pouch. Then she gently eased the heavy gold ear-ring out of his ear and put that with the gold dust.

'Now no one will recognize you,' she said. 'And we will spend the gold wisely when there is a time of need.'

Mau stretched and yawned then licked at her hand with his rough pink tongue. He shook his head delightedly. He had always hated that ear-ring.

Outside the sun was burning on the marshes, and Mau sniffed at the odorous air. There were wild fowl to chase and scare, birds to catch, fish to eat, mice to stalk and tease. He leaped out to begin a new dynasty.

Cats Do Make a Home, Don't They?

Judy Gardiner

Early evening was proceeding as usual in the Leamingtons' flat; regional news on the box and the sound of squawking and splashing in the bathroom. *Don't snatch the sponge away from Fenella, Timothy, when you can see she wants to play with it –*

A man in south-east London had been hiccoughing for fifty-seven days; Queens Park Rangers had suffered defeat and the price of crude oil was going up again. Leamington helped himself to a beer from the fridge before going through to the sittingroom. He turned off the television and sank into a chair with the *Guardian*. The front door bell rang.

He ignored it. Then, when it rang again, flung the paper aside and tramped through to the hall. A man of about his own age was standing on the doormat carrying a small suitcase and wearing an obsequious expression. Instantly divining that he was about to be sold something, Leamington gave a brisk smile and said that he never bought things on the spur of the moment.

'I'm sorry,' the man said, 'my name's Brand I live in the flat downstairs. The wife's gone off to her class and I've mislaid my key.'

'Oh.' Leamington hesitated. 'What a nuisance.'

'I don't suppose your key would fit our lock, would it?'

'Shouldn't think so. All Yale locks are supposed to be different, aren't they?'

They stood looking at one another doubtfully. Leamington began to wonder what the other bloke had got in his suitcase, while the man called Brand saw that Leamington was in his stockinged feet. They smiled a little feebly.

'You'd better come in,' Leamington conceded finally, 'and wait until your wife gets back.'

He led the way into the sittingroom and his eye fell upon the half empty beer glass.

'Drink?'

'Well . . . '

Leamington fetched another one. Offered it, then indicated that the man Brand should seat himself. Placing his burden carefully on the floor he did so, and Leamington saw that it was not a suitcase but a wicker basket.

'Our cat,' Brand said. 'Just been to fetch him from the vet.'

'We've got a cat,' Leamington said, seating himself opposite. 'One cat, two kids and a goldfish.'

'Well – cheers.'

'Cheers.'

They began to appraise one another with the polite caution of men who might consider becoming further acquainted. Brand was tall and sandy, with full lips and a rubbery nose. He was wearing a dark suit and striped shirt.

'We noticed you moving in,' Leamington said. 'Think you'll like it here?'

'It's smaller than we've been used to, but it cuts down commuting by half.'

'Personally,' Leamington said, 'the wife and I would rather have two smallish places than one big one. We've got a weekend cottage up in Suffolk.'

From out in the hall came the babble of child voices, the rapid padding of bare feet on carpet. The door flew open and two small children, pyjama'd and smelling of soap, bounded into the room.

'Say goodnight to Daddy,' said the blonde woman with her hair tied back and her sleeves rolled up. Noticing Brand, she gave him a casual smile.

The children engulfed Leamington, hitting him, kissing him and rumpling his hair.

'Goodnight! – I said *goodnight*! – ' Leamington came up for air. The blonde hauled the two children off and strolled away with one tucked under either arm.

'They look a pretty nice pair.'

'Yes,' Leamington stroked his hair down. 'In small doses. You got any?'

'Not yet,' said Brand.

A faint scratching followed by a plaintive mew came from the wicker basket at his feet. 'Okay Oscar, won't be long now.'

'That his name, Oscar?'

'Yes. After a chap we met in Yugoslavia on holiday.'

'Ours got called Kittypuss. A half Persian job.'

The blonde came back into the room, unrolling her sleeves.

'This is Mr Brand . . .' Leamington began, 'from the flat downstairs. Got himself locked out.'

'Bill Brand, glad to meet you,' said Brand, moving swiftly across the room to shake her hand. She smelt of the same soap as the children and he found himself appraising her long legs, neat little breasts and flat belly with sudden yearning.

'Nice to know you,' the blonde said, disengaging her hand without haste.

Leamington had poured a sherry for her and she had seated herself opposite Brand when her attention was caught by the basket at his feet.

'What's in there?'

'Our cat. I went to the vet to collect him and forgot my key, so I can't get in until the wife gets back from her class.'

'I've seen your wife,' Leamington's wife said. 'She looks nice.'

'I think she's noticed you, too.'

During the slight pause which followed, a fluffy black cat with tufts of fur growing out of its ears walked into the room and halted when it saw Brand. It stood considering him through orange-coloured eyes.

'Puss-puss,' chirped Brand, then remembered. 'Hi, Kittypuss, what's new?'

The cat began to stroll towards him, placing one forefoot before the other in a graceful, swaying movement. Then a slight scuffling sound from the basket made her freeze.

'All right, Kitters, old girl,' Leamington said, 'it's only Oscar. And you've got to be nice to Oscar because he's your new neighbour.'

Kittypuss remained motionless, then raised dilating nostrils in the direction of the basket. The orange of her eyes disappeared behind swelling black pupils.

'My family's always loved cats,' Leamington's wife said. 'At one time my mother had seven.'

'Interesting,' said Brand, and endeavoured to keep his eyes away from her small breasts and flat belly.

'But of course we had Kittypuss seen to – we both think its cruel to condemn her to a life of everlasting kittening . . .' Reaching behind her head she released the clip that fastened her hair. It fell forward in a golden shower which she shook back with a sensuous little movement of her head.

'Have another drink,' Leamington suggested, removing the empty glass from Brand's fingers.

'Well, I don't think the wife will be very long now.'

'What's the hurry? Stick a note on your front door telling her where you are.'

'I already have,' Brand confessed. 'But I don't want to impose on you.'

'Rubbish,' Leamington's wife said briskly. 'We were planning to ask you both in one evening, anyway.' She handed her empty glass to Leamington, who refilled it. 'How do you like living here?'

'Fine,' Brand said. 'The wife and I both feel we did the right thing.'

'And Oscar?' She leaned forward, staring through the chinks of the cat basket with one hand coiled round her ankle.

'No trouble with him at all. Didn't have to butter his paws or anything, did we, Osk ole boy?'

At the sound of his name the cat in the basket began to claw at the newspaper that lined the base. The basket rocked slightly.

'Let him out,' Leamington suggested. 'Kittypuss won't mind.'

Glasses in hand, they sat watching the female cat who had now retreated to the proximity of the coffee table. With tail curled and limbs tucked beneath her body she sat watching the basket with interest.

'Shall I?' Brand hesitated. 'He can't stand being cooped up.'

'What did he have to go to the vet for?' Leamington's wife asked.

'Oh – nothing infectious,' Brand fiddled with the straps that secured the lid of the basket. 'Just the usual, if you get me.'

'I get you,' she said, and at that moment the door opened a shade wider and a woman's head appeared round it.

141

'Oh – pardon me. The front door was on the latch and so I just . . .'

'Come in!' Leamington said heartily. 'Nice to meet you, Mrs er –'

'Brand,' said the woman, and walked smilingly into the room with hand outstretched. Tall and majestically radiant, it was immediately obvious that the class she had been attending was a pre-natal one.

Although the lid of the basket was wide open, the cat called Oscar made no immediate attempt to vacate it. He sat tensely upright while he surveyed the strange room, the four people in it, and the other cat crouching watchfully by the coffee table. He was a pale ginger with tabby markings the colour of vintage marmalade.

'I love cats,' the pregnant woman said, holding a glass of sherry. 'We always had them at home when I was a child.'

'I think cats *make* a home,' averred Leamington's wife. 'Like log fires and cosy slippers.'

'You haven't got open fires here, have you?' Brand's wife looked around.

'Oh, no, I was thinking about our cottage. The flat's electric.'

'Yes of course, so's ours.' They smiled at one another, gratified to discover two points in common within such a short while.

'I've seen you in the health food shop,' Leamington's wife said.

'Couldn't very well miss me, could you?'

'When's it due?'

'Early next month.'

'Lovely . . . Do you want a boy or a girl?'

'We honestly don't mind . . .'

The Leamingtons' cat continued to gaze at the one in the basket for a little while longer then abruptly stood up and left the room. She went out to the kitchen and began to eat the remainder of her supper; to tidy it away in case the other cat should come seeking it.

Back in the sitting room the ginger cat stepped out of the basket, sniffed at the Leamingtons' carpet and then climbed carefully on to Brand's lap. Brand rumpled its ears, and Leamington's wife smiled across at him and said: 'Why don't you both stay for a bite to eat? I made a pizza this afternoon and it's too big for just the two of us.'

The Brands began to demur, while glancing across at one another questioningly.

'Well, we ought to be going back – '

'Don't want to impose – '

'Ought to think about Oscar – '

'Oscar looks perfectly okay to me,' Leamington said, then stared openly for the first time at the big rounded belly of Brand's wife. 'And some of us here have got to keep up our strength, haven't we?'

'You're dead right,' Brand said, grinning. 'It takes a lot of effort being an expectant father.'

'Look,' Leamington's wife said from the door. 'Your part's over now.'

They all laughed, and knew that they were on the brink of becoming friends, and while Leamington brought in two bottles of supermarket chianti his wife piled plates and salad and pizza and biscuits and cheese on the trolley and wheeled it in from the kitchen. And the cat Oscar shuffled a little on Brand's lap, trying to find a comfortable spot for the sore place where its testicles had been.

The rattle of forks, the tinkle of glasses. The happy picnic atmosphere of eating on laps in unexpected and congenial company. Brand now in shirt sleeves.

'Timothy arrived in a flash but Fenella was a breech birth.'

'We did breech births at our class last week. Does it really make much difference?'

'No, not really. So long as the doctor knows what he's doing,' Leamington's wife said, munching a radish.

'I'm being induced.'

'Any special reason?'

'Oh, no. Except that my doctor doesn't believe in prolonging things unnecessarily.'

'That's enlightened of him.'

'And he'll be on holiday when it's actually due.'

'Ah. So when . . .?'

'We've decided on the 3rd. It's a Friday, and my husband thinks he can take the day off.'

'Make a long weekend of it.'

'Yes, that's what we thought.'

Kittypuss came back into the room, covertly licking her lips. Swaying over to the sofa where the two women were sitting she jumped onto Leamington's wife's lap.

'No, Kitsy – not while there's food about . . . '

'I'm afraid we let Oscar sleep on our bed.'

'Yes – we're a bit the same. Trouble is, they share your life and it's difficult not to think of them as human beings, too.'

'Oh, Oscar's absolutely one of us. I do hope he won't feel jealous when the baby comes.'

'I don't suppose he will. Cats are amazingly intelligent and he'll soon understand that it's your kitten.'

'My kitten,' said Brand's wife, discreetly caressing her belly. 'What a lovely way to think of it.'

When they had finished the biscuits and cheese Leamington passed round the last of the chianti.

'I shouldn't really,' Brand's wife said. 'It gives me heartburn.'

'If I may say so,' Leamington said very formally, 'I think you're looking absolutely sublime.'

'Well – thank you.' She smiled, and held out her glass.

And as if Leamington had just passed a remark of extraordinary perception, a hush fell on the conversation and the room seemed to become filled for a moment with a sense of the powerfully primaeval. Sublime was the only possible word to describe not only Brand's wife, but also the condition she represented. No one moved except Kittypuss, who slid quietly from her owner's lap on to that of the pregnant woman. In comparison it was no more than a narrow ledge, but she lay against the tightly packed drum of the baby, purring and gently kneading it with her paws.

'What did I tell you?' Leamington's wife whispered. 'They understand far more than we give them credit for.'

She slipped from the room to make some coffee.

While the kettle boiled she returned with a saucer of milk.

'We've been forgetting poor Oscar. Come on, Oscar old boy . . . come on and have some milkies . . . '

Lithe as a dancer she placed the saucer on the carpet in front of Brand's feet. The cat Oscar made as if to run, and Brand, stroking him, thought Christ, that woman's body. She can't weigh more than eight and a half, and everything's perfect. And yet she's had two pregnancies.

'Go on, Osk,' he said aloud. 'Go and see what's in the saucer.'

He placed the cat on the floor, and everyone including Kittypuss watched as he stood awkwardly, stiffly, with his tail held as if it didn't belong to him.

'Come on, Oscar,' wheedled Leamington's wife, sitting at Brand's feet and tilting the saucer invitingly.

Warily the cat approached, sniffed tentatively, then subjected everyone in the room to a slow penetrating stare before finally settling to drink.

'It's a rotten business, going to the vet,' Brand's wife said in a low voice.

'Do you have him immunized every year?'

'Oh, yes.'

'So do we. It costs a small fortune, but we love her so much we think she's worth it.'

'Catteries won't take them for the holidays unless they've got their certificates of immunization, will they?'

'I know. Sometimes I wonder if it isn't all a bit of a racket, but if anything happened . . .'

'Exactly. They're part of our lives, and we treat them like ourselves . . .'

Quietly and without haste Kittypuss left Brand's wife's lap and poured herself over the arm of the sofa. Taking a circuitous route behind the music centre she approached the other cat, who was lapping at the milk with his eyes closed. Leamington showed signs of interfering, but his wife raised her hand: 'No – leave them.'

He did so, and Kittypuss moved out from the shadow of the coffee table and approached Oscar from the rear. With dilated eyes and nostrils she took in the scent of him, then moved closer until her nose touched his body. His eyes flew open and he sprang sideways.

'He *spat* at her! – ' someone laughed.

'Oh Oscar, how rude – and in someone else's home, too! . . .'

With calm deliberation Kittypuss addressed herself to the saucer, and with her tail tucked tidily round her body crouched to drink the last of the milk while the intruder stood watching. Then he sat down, carefully, and waited to see what would happen next.

Glasses and coffee cups empty. Crumbs on the floor and a lazy feeling of repletion. The Leamingtons and the Brands felt as if they had been friends for years.

'You going to be there?'

'What – when it's born? Oh, yes.'

'I was with the wife when both of ours arrived.'

'Bit of a business, I gather?' Brand eyed Leamington with a mixture of caution and curiosity.

'Something you'll never forget, I'll say that,' Leamington said, and wanted, sentimentally, to add something to the effect that in this cold technological world a pregnant woman's something real; something to grasp hold of, as it were. But lethargy prevented it and he decided to let Brand find out for himself.

'More coffee?' Leamington's wife approached them, holding out her hands for their cups. They declined, and Brand thought how beautiful she must have looked when she was pregnant. Sublime, yes, that was the word.

'A woman in our pre-natal class wants to be delivered on all fours,' Brand's wife confided.

Reseated beside her, Leamington's wife brushed her long blonde hair back and said: 'Gosh, I envy you. You've no idea how I envy you, right this minute.'

Her voice drifted on the still air. The two men smiled dreamily.

Summer twilight brought lilac-tinted shadows, and from the lee of Brand's chair Kittypuss stared deep into the eyes of Oscar then stood up and walked unobtrusively behind the sofa. Unobtrusively he followed her.

In quiet seclusion they at last began a detailed examination of one another, noses touching, whiskers mingling. With one paw ready to strike she sniffed his ears and he stood patiently while her gently bobbing nose continued down his back and then hesitated for a moment at the brutal smell of disinfectant. There was still a little dried blood, and she cleaned it for him carefully. He growled, but allowed her to finish.

Already he was becoming accustomed to her own scent; in it, he could read what had also been done to her for her own benefit, and as a sad little token of acceptance he brushed the side of his cheek against her neck. They sat down together, feet tucked beneath them; two well-loved, well-tended little empty vessels.

'Did you say delivered on all fours?' Leamington's wife suddenly broke the silence on the other side of the sofa. 'My God – just like an animal.'

Samkin

Mark Ronson

I am Samkin.

I am very black and I used to be heavy, but since taking to the woods I have become lean. The tabby over at Hollow Oak Farm sneered at me some nights ago for being skin and bone. All right for her to talk, with food every morning and warm ashes to sleep beside every night.

Still, I survive – though I cannot pounce as fast as I could in my early days. There was a time I could claw up a tree and catch a thrush before it spread its wings. Now I have to work hard to catch a young rabbit. And the days are getting colder . . .

Sometimes at night, curled up in bracken, I dream I am back in Mistress Marten's cottage, purring dutifully on the old woman's lap while she tells me about her young days.

I liked her from the moment she took me from the litter at the miller's. She was lonely and spoke to me a great deal, which is why I have a good understanding of human talk. My meals were regular, and she was kind to other animals. In winter she threw crusts out for the birds – until she saw that I stalked them for sport.

Mistress was very clever at mixing herbs to cure sickness, just as we cats know the right grass to nibble at certain times. Humans from the village walked to the cottage to ask for medicines.

'My grandma taught me how to prepare physics and salves,' she would say. 'Sorry am I that I've no grandchild to give my recipes to.' Then she would look unhappy the way humans do when their eyes rain. 'Alack, my son Robin died of the Sweating Sickness at the same time as his father – may they both rest in peace.'

Sometimes I followed her to the big house they call church. Stone crosses grew in its garden and, putting flowers on two earth mounds there, she would talk quietly though I could see no one. When we returned home I knew she was sad because she gave me more attention than usual. After supper she sat by the fire and stroked me and talked on and on. Sometimes she said, 'What an old simpleton I be – talking to a poor dumb creature with no notion of speech.'

She did not realize I understood much of what she said. Most humans have under-rated our intelligence since the ancient days when cats and men made their bargain – to guard grain in return for shelter and milk.

When I was still a kitten Mistress had a few friends – old women like herself – who came to the cottage to drink a medicine which smelled like apples. Then they would laugh and giggle about things which happened long ago, but, as I grew older, fewer came and Mistress made more visits to the church garden. For the last two years no friends called, only young girls knocking on the door after dark for what they called 'love potions' or a mother wanting a draught for her child. And even such visits became fewer.

'I need something for the ague, good mistress,' said one of the last women to come. 'But please do not tell that I use such medication for it would go ill with me in the village.'

'Why?' asked Mistress. 'For years the village has come to me.'

''Tis the minister. He be that strong on what be right and wrong. All his talk be about sin and hellfire and the wrath of God. From the pulpit he says that herbals be the lure of Satan and only prayer can heal, but I have prayed and my man is no better.'

'He's young and from the town,' said Mistress. 'He'll learn country ways in time. Old Parson – God rest him – used to see me when he needed a purge, and there was no tattle of the Devil then.'

Soon afterwards Mistress had a quarrel with Timothy Wandyke, who owned the field next to our cottage, and it was the start of our troubles.

I remember opening an eye early that morning to see Mistress putting her cloak over her shoulders.

'Be thee coming with me, Samkin?' she asked. ''Tis a fine morning for picking herbs with dew still upon them.'

I uncurled from my box of straw by the hearth and decided to go. A vole or a harvest mouse might cross my path, and I always enjoyed ambling behind her while she prattled. Like most cats, I have no objection to human attention even when it is just the sound of a voice.

We set off along the hedgerows and soon Mistress had plucked enough plants to fill her basket.

'Here be wood-sorrel, Samkin,' she said. 'It makes a fine cordial for the heart. And here wild borage. Look, Samkin, its flowers are like little blue stars which distil into a lotion for smoothing wrinkles. And here be wolfbane – we be needing none of that . . .' So she prattled while I rolled in delight at exciting scents which came from her basket.

'What be you doing in my field, beldame?'

The unexpected voice was so full of anger that I jumped into the hedgerow while Mistress straightened up with her hands full of greenery.

Standing behind her was a burly man I knew as Timothy Wandyke.

'Why, Tim, you sound full of choler this fine morning.'

'Ay, that be so when I see a bitch-hag who the parson preaches agin walking my land.'

'But, Tim, for years thy father has let me pick herbs in this paddock for my simples.'

'My father be a dotard, and I'll not aid Devil's work so get thee gone.'

'Timothy Wandyke, what harm have I done? When thee were small and had the coughing fever it was me that cured thee. Is it because I will not sell my little orchard to thee?'

For a moment the big human did not know what to say. Then he seized her basket and strewed the herbs over the turf. Mistress began to walk back to her cottage, calling 'Samkin, Samkin!' I left the shelter of the hedge and followed her with my tail up to show I scorned the farmer's anger.

'And keep your God-cursed familiar away,' he shouted. 'I'll have no Satan spawn here.'

He threw his cudgel which caught me on the back leg. I leapt into the air spitting, then limped off as fast as I could.

'As with this creature, so be it with you,' Mistress cried. 'And may you cry for one of my cures!'

In the cottage she scooped yellow cream off the milk as a treat for me, and put me on her knee so I could not help purring even though my leg pained.

'Eh, Samkin,' she said, rubbing my ear in a way I loved. 'Eh Samkin, the world is leaving me behind.'

Soon news spread that Timothy Wandyke was limping after his bull had gored him, and that his youngest child was sick with Spotted Fever. But his wife did not come across the field for a remedy as she would have done once. Mistress, who seemed to become more frail and bent, shunned the village, though once she went down the lane to the church garden with flowers.

As she reached the gate some lads shouted a word which was new to me, although soon I was to hear it often.

'Witch!'

One knocked the posy from her hands, and another was just picking up a stone when Teacher – a young human new to the village – ran up and sent them away. When she got home Mistress picked me up and I felt her heart fluttering like a bird when you carry it in your mouth.

'Oh, black Samkin, in all the world thee be all I have left,' she whispered. I tried to make her feel better by kneading her with my paws, but over her shoulder I saw something move at the window. Against the sunlight was the shape of a human head which vanished suddenly – and I foresaw something terrible would happen soon. Although I pride myself on understanding humans as well as the next cat – perhaps better because I am more intelligent than most – I had no idea what this would be, and I did not understand it even when it came upon us. It was human business and I can only tell what took place.

Next day I sat in my lair among sweet-smelling bushes when humans came up the lane and my tail tingled at the sight of them. There was Parson with Timothy Wandyke limping beside him, and a stranger with very large dark eyes, fur on his chin and hair that fell to his shoulders from beneath a tall hat. He wore a black cloak over black doublet and breeches, and his riding boots were soft leather with spurs still on them. In his hand he held a long staff.

Behind him came a human with a face which reminded me of a

150

fox, and a big woman who walked with a man's stride. A group of villagers followed at a distance, nudging each other and pointing at the strangers.

They stopped outside our cottage and waited, Parson talking so excitedly to the Man in Black that spittle speckled his chin. From the opposite direction came the clopping of a horse and up rode red-faced Magistrate who only seemed happy when galloping over the fields. Now he looked as though he would rather be somewhere else. Earlier I had seen mounted humans setting out to kill animals and I guessed he wanted to ride with them.

'Well, Parson,' he said. 'What's all this damned nonsense, hey?'

'I wish for the sake of sweet Jesu Christ that it was nonsense, Sir Richard,' replied Parson. 'But there is danger to our salvation here and for help in this peril I summoned the Witch-Finder General.'

The Man in Black bowed.

'Matthew Hopkins, at your service,' he said. 'Permit me to introduce my devoted assistant John Stearne and my pricker Goody Phillips. For the sake of decency it is she who seeks for the Devil's Mark in the secret places of females accused.'

Magistrate muttered something about 'damned Puritans' and dismounted.

'Still think it's a lot of nonsense,' he said. 'The old dame is a bit strange in the belfrey but that comes to us all with age.'

'You wouldn't say that if you had been overlooked and your child lay in the cold earth,' began Timothy Wandyke angrily, but Parson hushed him, saying, 'You'll have your turn to . . .'

'I trust, Sir Richard, that you do not doubt the existence of the Devil's converts,' interrupted the Man in Black. 'To do so would be to deny the existence of the Devil and by implication the existence of God.'

'I meant no blasphemy,' said Magistrate hurriedly. 'How much is this mummery costing the parish?'

'Sir, fees are modest,' answered the Man in Black, his dark eyes flashing angry. 'For visiting a village my charge is merely twenty shillings, out of which I must pay expenses and maintain my company with three horses. Then, for each conviction I receive a further twenty shillings.'

'Ay, I heard you earned £23 over at Stowmarket.'

151

'Stowmarket was sore afflicted. But my father was a man of the cloth and I am happy to follow his example by doing the Lord's work in my chosen way.'

'Then let's get on with the Lord's work.'

Parson hammered on our door and shouted: 'Mistress Marten, I summon you to open to us in the name of God.'

The door slowly opened and they went inside. While the villagers crowded round the threshold, I climbed in the little window at the back so I could watch through a crack in the pantry door.

Mistress was milk white and lay back in her chair by the fire. The Man in Black, Stearne and Goody Phillips stood against the wall while Magistrate unfolded a paper which Parson had given him.

'Jane, I wish to God I did not have to read this to you,' he said. 'But it is my legal duty and I promise that you shall be tried legal. You are charged on the following counts –

'Item: That you have made potions for magical use.

'Item: That you have cast spells to cure ailments, a Devilish trick which will be revealed on Judgement Day when the resurrected shall see their afflicted parts so healed putrify.'

Magistrate turned with a puzzled look to Parson who nodded and said, 'So teaches the Church.'

'Item: That you have been seen by named witnesses to commune with the dead in the graveyard,' Magistrate continued.

'Item: That you have overlooked one Timothy Wandyke so that he was lamed and his child sickened unto death.'

I did not understand this 'item' talk, but my ears pricked up when I heard my name.

'And finally, Mistress Jane Marten, that you do keep a famulus in the shape of a black cat which you call Samkin and that you give him suck from a Devil's Pap.

'If you cannot answer these charges, I have no choice but to authorize Matthew Hopkins, known as the Witch-Finder General, to test you as to your innocence or guilt. What say you?'

While Magistrate had been reading the paper Mistress had buried her head in her hands, and I could tell by the way her shoulders shook that she was making rain on her face. But now she looked straight at them.

'Untruth – 'tis all untruth,' she said in a low voice. 'You all know

152

that I have made simples, and my mother before me, and until now no word has been said against it. Think you of the cures they have worked. And why should I be blamed because Tim Wandyke has a bull which he knew was savage ever since it gored old Joseph the cowman. Nor can I be blamed for the death of his Emily – who I might have been able to cure had I been asked. And why call me witch because I have a cat now that I am old and alone and have none else to talk to . . .'

'Ah,' said the Man in Black with a smile. 'You admit that you hold converse with your famulus.'

Mistress became confused as he began shouting questions at her. When she was unable to answer him, Parson and the man Stearne looked at each other as though they were pleased about something, and Goody Phillips rubbed her hands behind her back. The villagers listened open-mouthed and whenever the Man in Black drew breath after saying something they cried 'Ah' as though they had known it all along.

At last the Man in Black turned to Magistrate and Parson and said, 'Gentlemen, I declare there are grounds for a proper investigation and if it prove that this woman has made a Satanic pact, then be she sentenced according to law . . .'

''Tis rubbish you speak,' came a new voice and everyone turned as Teacher pushed his way in. 'Mistress Marten has spent over three score years in this village and who has been harmed by her – and who has she not helped with her balms? So what is her crime, may I ask? That she speaks to her cat! But is that so unusual? Sir Richard, do you not speak words to your hunter or hound?'

Magistrate slapped his boot with his crop.

'Mr Schoolmaster, I am a simple squire and out of my depth here. But to give an honest answer, of course I speak encouragement to Caesar in the field . . .'

'Holy Writ states, "thou shalt not suffer a witch to live" – Exodus twenty-two, verse eighteen,' cried Parson.

'It seems 'tis the Old Testament you love the best,' said Teacher. 'Yet I cannot see Our Saviour seeking the execution of women in the dotage . . .'

The villagers began shouting, sounding as they do when watching cocks fight. Then the Man in Black held up both his arms and said in

153

a commanding way, 'Pray no more argument. Goody Phillips, begin the examination.

The big woman pulled Mistress to her feet.

'Undo your gown, madam,' she said.

Mistress did not seem to understand the words so Goody Phillips tore her clothing so that she stood in her shift. This was pulled down so that mistress was bare to the waist, and a laugh came from the doorway.

'Hast though seen such long dugs!'

'Something heavy has swung on them.'

'Old Nick most like.'

Mistress tried to cross her hands across her chest and her face had colour again.

The Man in Black took out a long needle and offered it to Goody Phillips.

'No need for pricking, Master Hopkins,' she said, and she forced Mistress' arm above her head.

'There,' she cried. 'The Witch Pap.' And with her free hand she pointed to a mark which humans call a mole on her side.

There was a frightened murmur from the villagers, but Teacher stepped forward.

'Before God,' he cried, 'this is the seventeenth century! What one of you here does not have a wart or piles, and be you all witches!'

'Goody has such experience that she can tell the difference between a wart and a Devil's Teat,' said the Man in Black.

'No conviction without confession,' muttered Magistrate.

'Sir, I worked at the law in Ipswich before I took up the burden of Witch-Finder General,' said the Man in Black. 'There will be further investigation – for I be a fair man – and when we know for certain I doubt not that you shall have your confession. Pray, Master Parson, lead us to your mill pond.'

Goody Phillips and the man Stearne dragged my mistress out of the cottage. Everyone from the village seemed to be outside and all set off to the mill, singing and laughing as they did on the way to the summer fair. I stalked along the ditch and often I saw Mistress stumble. In a cracked voice she begged Goody Phillips to let her rest.

'Let her draw breath and cover her nakedness,' said Magistrate. 'I doubt me not that the pond will still be there a few minutes from now.'

Mistress sat on the bank and panted while Teacher ran back to the cottage and brought a blanket which he wrapped round her. The villagers sent to the inn for jugs of ale.

I crept through the long grass as close as I dared and Mistress caught sight of me.

'Samkin,' she cried. 'Shoo, Samkin!'

I vanished into some bushes as shouting started.

'She's calling upon her imp!'

'I see him,' a woman shrieked, nodding in the wrong direction. 'Eyes like coals and two heads he have – and the Devil's hoof.'

Most humans crowded back. Several young girls pointed to a tree and swore that they saw something with bat's wings on the top branch.

'Enough of foolery,' growled Magistrate. 'Let us have done with this miserable business.'

At the mill pond the Man in Black said, 'If Mistress Marten be guilty the water will reject her and she will float. If she be innocent she will sink like any child of God, and we will save her with ropes.'

Goody Phillips made Mistress lie on the bank and the man Stearne tied her big toes to her thumbs with twine, and then tied two ropes to her waist. While the Man in Black held one rope, he pulled her into the water with the other. For a moment she went under and then appeared on the surface with duckweed in her hair.

'She floats!' was the cry. And she did not sink, but I think it was because of the way the two humans held the ropes.

'She is guilty as is writ in King James's book on the nature of witchcraft,' said Parson.

Mistress was dragged back to the village where everyone went into the corn hall. I knew it well, having caught many a rat there among the great bags of grain. So it was not difficult for me to climb through a secret gap beneath the eaves to the gallery where I could look down on everybody.

Mistress sat alone at one end of the hall, her poor old body shivering in her wet shift. The humans stood crowded at the other end, while in the centre Magistrate sat at a table with a book in front of him and a quill in his hand with which he sometimes picked his teeth.

'Mistress Marten,' he said quietly. 'I call upon you to confess to the crime of witchcraft, and to tell for the record the nature of your pact with Lucifer.'

Mistress managed to say, 'I have nothing to confess – who have I done harm to?'

'Me and mine,' shouted Timothy Wandyke. 'You sent your imp – Sumpkin or whatever you call him – to poison my child . . .'

'And it were her that blighted my oats,' cried another farmer.

'One at a time,' said Magistrate. 'You first, Farmer Wandyke, and speak slow because I am a poor hand at pencraft.'

Timothy Wandyke told how he had seen Mistress in his field gathering herbs for unholy spells with her familiar, and how she had cursed him so that he went lame.

I could not help yawning in my hiding place as he was followed by others who had tales to tell about Mistress. Even a girl who had come a few nights earlier for a love charm described how Mistress spoke to me and I had answered her. Of course I often gave her a 'miaow', and I could not understand what the fuss was about.

I washed my fur and dozed until I was woken by the angry voice of Teacher demanding that Mistress be set free.

'There is no confession,' he cried.

'That will come,' said the Man in Black.

'Ay, if you torment her enough,' said Teacher. 'But I understand, Master Witch-Finder, that there is yet another test which is held to be infallible, and conclusive by law, and I say that if you truly believe in the powers of evil you will be willing to be bound by this as to her guilt.'

'What is this test?' Magistrate asked.

'It has been said at witch trials that a famulus will always return to her who gives it suck, even if she be sealed in a room which no living being can enter. Therefore let us keep Mistress Marten here, with every entry sealed, and see if her imp will materialize while we keep vigil, and if no famulus appears I say she should be released.'

'Do you agree, Master Hopkins?' asked Magistrate, and he smiled for the first time.

The Man in Black whispered with Stearne, then nodded.

'Those who wish can stay here the night and watch,' said Magistrate standing up, 'and I shall return after breaking my fast.'

'Search the hall so that we be certain there is no creature already here,' said Parson as Magistrate walked into the dusk. The villagers made a great business of locking the doors and making sure the shutters were closed. Many were swaying as humans do when they have been drinking what they call ale. When they came up to the gallery I had no difficulty in hiding from them – a black cat is hard to see in the shadows.

Mistress was placed in the centre of the floor by the table with a lamp on it while Parson knelt in front of her with his hands pressed together and talked very loud to someone he called 'O Lord'.

Mistress moaned to herself and sometimes the man Stearne gripped her shoulder and said, 'Confess, dame, and make it easy for us all, for 'twill be the same in the end.' She only shook her head.

How I wished I was back in our cottage with Mistress skimming my cream but I knew – in the way that we cats know these things – that such happy evenings were over for ever. But even a cat cannot alter fate and after a while I dozed in the shadow.

It was the sound of crying which roused me. I stretched, crept down the stairs and jumped on to Mistress' lap, purring and pushing with my paws.

'Samkin!'

I replied with the usual loud 'miaow'.

'Sweet Christ, preserve our souls!'

Turning my head I saw the humans had woken and were jumping to their feet.

'Her guilt is proven,' cried the Man in Black. 'Her famulus has become manifest.'

'I exorcise thee, imp of Satan,' chanted Parson. 'Begone thou hideous demon unto thine appointed place and return no more to plague the Servants of Almighty God.'

Frightened, I leapt on to the table and upset the lamp so that night filled the hall. Darkness is the friend of cats, and while I heard flints being struck I raced up the stairs.

'Samkin has come and gone as we all witnessed, woman,' the Man in Black said when the lamp flickered into life again. 'Ease yourself by confession.'

Goody Phillips and the man Srearne seized Mistress by the arms and began running up and down the hall with her. She lost her

157

footing so they dragged her backwards and forwards like millers hauling grain sacks. Up and down, up and down they pulled her until she agreed to what they asked.

'Did you put a laming spell on Master Timothy?' asked the Man in Black.

'Anything . . . but let me be.'

'And did you send Samkin to poison his child Emily . . . you do not deny it?'

There was a sigh from the watchers as Mistress dropped her head.

I left by the hole under the eaves and went to our cottage. In the moonlight I saw the door swinging open, the little windows I used to look out of when I was a kitten were smashed, and inside everything had been taken away. There was no food and I knew that from then on I must become a hunter.

Soon after dawn I woke in a ditch. It was not the song of birds which had roused me but the sound of boots on the frosty road. Looking through clumps of willow-herb I saw a procession of villagers. Mistress staggered along between the man Stearne and Goody Phillips while Parson and the Man in Black walked behind Magistrate's horse.

I followed behind hedgerows until we came to the crossroads where men had set up a wooden post around which had been heaped straw, faggots and small logs. Mistress shivered while the black-smith fastened her to the post by a chain.

On his horse Magistrate unrolled a paper and read in a strangely shaky voice: 'Mistress Marten, by your own confession you have committed the crime of witchcraft. Further, you have admitted that by means magical you have poisoned one Emily Wandyke.

'Therefore, by the law of this land, you shall be executed by fire, not for the crime of witchcraft which in England does not carry this penalty as in Popish lands, but for the crime of poisoning which is rightly regarded as the greatest of all crimes save treason, and which carries the penalty of burning. Therefore I authorize your punishment . . .'

He rolled up the paper and looked down at Parson and the Man in Black.

'Now sirs, to your task.' And he galloped away over the field.

'There is one thing I would say before this lawful execution is carried out,' said the Man in Black. 'It is my experience that when one witch is found there are others close by, for it is the nature of witches to form covens to worship their infernal master in grave-yards and in Druid rings. And I tell you that I smell more evil here.'

A nervous murmur came from the humans.

'So my assistants and I shall remain here at our own expense until all witches have been discovered. And think you not that they are all beldames like Mistress Marten. Witchcraft transcends sex and con-dition, and you may have heard tell that at Brandeston I had the confession of John Lowes, the minister, that he did send a famulus to sink a ship at sea.

'I warn you to be on your guard, and if you see aught strange in your neighbour give me news of it privily.'

He stepped back and Parson stood below Mistress on her pile of wood.

'I give you a last chance to repent,' he said, holding up his black book.

'I am cold, sir,' said Mistress. 'Please spare me a little warmth . . . and let me go home for Samkin will be wanting his milk.'

Several laughed, and then the world seemed to fill with silence as Blacksmith struck a spark on to a torch and lit straw near Mistress's feet. She leaned forward and held her hands out to the heat.

'Thankee, good sir,' she said.

Blacksmith went round the bundles of straw with his torch and then stood back as fire danced round Mistress so that I could only see her head and shoulders. Her mouth was open but I heard no sound through the flame roar. Then her hair began to blaze.

When not hunting I thought about what had happened. It seemed to me that the human who had caused the death of my mistress was Parson. It was he who had spoken against her and had called in the Man in Black who now remained in the village. But in a way I could not understand I felt I was also to blame. If I had not gone to her that night the humans might not have burned her. They had been afraid of me, and I realized that this gave me power.

That day I crept to the church garden where some people lowered a box into the ground. They had rain on their faces and Parson read

159

from his black book. I jumped up on one of the mossy stones and looked at him with my green eyes wide. When he lowered his book his voice faded so that the humans looked at him in surprise. He drew his hand across his eyes, and when he looked again I was hidden behind the stone.

From then on I made sure that he often glimpsed me. Once I followed him into church where he was muttering in front of a table with a cross on it. I sat on it, so that when he opened his eyes he saw me.

'Cease to haunt me, creature of evil,' he shouted, looking fearfully round the church.

'Sweet lord, if anyone saw this . . .' he said, and threw the black book at me.

When the day came on which the bells ring, I went to the church when the villagers were inside and slipped through the side door which Parson used. Here I was in a small room with another door open enough for me to see into the church.

Parson was sitting in his chair while the Man in Black talked to the people.

'Last night two more failed the pricking test – the needle went into their flesh without paining them,' he said. 'As yet they have not passed on the name of their black priest who presides at their sabbats, but sooner or later I shall find the leader for I shall not rest until this evil is rooted out.'

As he continued the humans gazed at him with frightened eyes, and often Parson cried 'Amen!' in a loud voice.

Then I knew exactly what I must do.

I ran into church and jumped into Parson's lap, rubbing my head against his face.

'Samkin!' cried several voices in horror.

Parson jumped to his feet, but I clung to his shoulder and gave a loud 'miaow'.

'The famulus returns from Hell,' the Man in Black shouted.

I fled to the door and, looking back, saw the Man in Black point his staff at Parson. Blacksmith and some others closed on him, and the man Stearne gave Goody Phillips a secret wink.

Parson has gone now, and I still live in the woods.

160